300

- ED.

D1175691

# Danger! Marines at Work!

Robert G. Fuller

# Danger!

# Marines

# at Work!

 Random House, New York

© Copyright, 1957, 1958, 1959, by Popular Publications, Inc.
First Printing

© Copyright, 1959, by Robert G. Fuller

All rights reserved under International and Pan-American
Copyright Conventions. Published in New York by
Random House, Inc., and simultaneously in Toronto,
Canada, by Random House of Canada, Limited.

Library of Congress Catalog Card Number: 59-5723

Manufactured in the United States of America
by The Colonial Press Inc., Clinton, Mass.

# Danger! Marines at Work!

# 1.

When Major Harold Barrow, U.S.M.C., reported to General Burgermeister's command headquarters in Nouméa, New Caledonia, it caused a sensation. Clerks, runners, paymasters, quartermasters, cooks and bakers—all the officers and men who weren't on guard—flocked to the giant Quonset for a glimpse of Major Barrow. They had already nicknamed him "Killer"—this brave Marine who was to take over the command of the First Parachute Battalion.

"He's got eyes of ice," a captain whispered to a lieutenant.

"He looks like Captain Bligh," a first sergeant told a sergeant major.

"He's a fat old slob," one private told another.

"Still, he must be the toughest officer in the Corps," a regimental runner said to the privates.

"Yeah," one of the privates agreed. "Washington must have a lot of respect for him to make him skipper of the paratroopers."

"Or he's number one on their nasty list," the other private suggested.

"Anyway," the runner spoke what they all knew to be the truth, "they'll make him a colonel if he tames those beasts up at Tontouta."

Major Harold Barrow certainly did not look like a lion tamer. Carrying a brief case and dressed in a neatly pressed forest-green stateside uniform, which clashed with the informal khaki and green twill fatigues of the Marines around the command post, he looked more like an insurance salesman or a real-estate agent than a two-fisted commanding officer.

Once, ten years before, girls did not look at Harold Barrow and giggle. They looked at him and sighed, because, in those days, like the Marines on the recruiting posters, he had been trim and rugged and handsome and carried himself proudly erect and walked with a cocky swagger. He had been a professional hockey player and had worn his lean hardness like a plume.

Now he waddled. He certainly was no longer trim. Ten years in Washington—behind a desk in the auditor's office and long hours on a stool with his fellow chairborne officers in the Mayflower Bar—had broadened him and spread him into a series of bulges which gave him a shape like a milk bottle.

The once broad, strong shoulders had been padded and rounded by layers of excess calories, and the long legs that had taken him over the twenty-mile forced marches had grown thicker than his waist used to be. He no longer had a waist at all. A fistful of suet overlapped his belt, hiding it, and brought his hips out in remarkable and unlovely relief.

Even his face had changed in the more than one hundred months since the order from headquarters had required him to put his rifle aside in favor of a fountain pen. The space between his prominent cheekbones and the line of his square jaw had filled out, leaving him with a moon face. But the soft life had not reached his eyes. They were still clear and blue, inquisitive and intelligent. They were quick to betray anger and equally quick to indicate his capacity for generosity and friendliness. Unfortunately, the nature of his work—the scrutiny of detailed accounts and the checking of long lists of figures—had afflicted him with a squint that made him look like a friendly owl.

The major had gone to seed; and compared to the physical specimens he was to lead, Barrow would look more like an aging student reporting to the gym master for reconditioning than a dashing, dauntless Marine hero.

General Burgermeister was not impressed by Major Barrow; he had just finished reading the major's service record. With his aide, Colonel Ward, he watched with a look of deep disappointment on his face as Barrow entered his office, sloppily executed a left-and-right-face and assumed what was supposed to be the position of attention before his desk.

"Major Harold Barrow reporting for duty, sir."

"So you're the formidable Major Barrow," Burgermeister said, disconsolately running a hamlike hand over his square, jutting jaw and breathing a sigh of disgust from deep in his barrel chest. "The new commanding officer of the First Parachute Battalion."

"Yes, sir," Barrow answered eagerly. "And I want to tell you how much I appreciate having been awarded this wonderful assignment."

"An award, is it?" the sardonic, tough old general mused. "That's a new twist."

"Yes, sir. I had my name on the list for transfer to a combat unit for eight years. I never thought I'd be made

the commander of the finest outfit in the Pacific theater
—in the whole Marine Corps," Barrow said enthusiasti-
cally.

"Is he talking about the First Parachute Battalion?"
Colonel Ward wanted to know.

"I certainly am, sir," Barrow said, delighted at the
thought of associating with the men of that splendid combat team. "The First Parachute Battalion holds the record for decorations for heroism and promotions for
conduct in battle. Why, on Gavutu . . ."

"We know, Major," Burgermeister interrupted. "We
were there. But of more immediate importance is the
condition of the battalion today. You will have your
work cut out for you as commanding officer of that outfit. It needs tightening up. The paratroopers do not seem
to take this period of retraining very seriously and I need
them on the next push, which is coming up very soon. I
depend on you to . . ."

"You can depend on me, sir," Barrow assured the general. "With the fine record of accomplishment they
earned in the Solomons, it shouldn't take long to get those
battle-hardened men back into tiptop shape."

"Never underestimate the enemy," Colonel Ward said
sourly.

Burgermeister decided to change tactics. Barrow's
preconceived notions about the paratroopers seemed to
have built up an impregnable enthusiasm. The general
wanted to get his message across to this man who would
lead the important hit-and-run parachutists.

"According to your folder, Barrow," he began, hard-
ening his voice, "although you once showed promise as
Marine officer material, several years ago you let yourself get shelved in the auditor's office of the paymaster's

department, and there you would have died in obscurity if this war had not come along. Therefore, this assignment almost constitutes a promotion for you."

"Thank you, sir." Barrow beamed. "I am fully aware of the great responsibility and honor bestowed on me and I will work very hard to justify your faith in me."

"Of course," Burgermeister said, gritting his teeth and trying to be patient. "But regardless of your conception of this detail, it will prove to be tough duty. If you are successful in whipping the battalion back into the combat team it once was, in time for the next hit, I will give you a fitness report that will make them take notice of you back in Washington and qualify you for excellent field commands. However, I must caution you that other fine officers have tackled this job and failed."

"What happened to them, sir?"

"One had a nervous breakdown. Two are waiting for their court-martial. The M.P.s are looking for the one who went over the hill."

"Oh."

"Don't forget the one in the strait jacket," Ward added.

"You are a regular, not a nation-saver, Barrow," Burgermeister went on, "and you have a dozen years in this lash-up. You never were a pusher, and as a result you got a lot of colorless jobs which have added up to a very unspectacular career for a Marine officer. I hope you will be able to take advantage of the opportunity this situation offers you."

"I surely will, sir," the major replied. "And I thank you for your interest in me."

"Interest in you, my foot!" the general exploded. "The only interest I have in you is the possibility that you might get that battalion into condition for a beach party. I need them. They're fighting fools, but they're battle-wacky and falling apart. If you can do the job, you're my man."

"Yes, sir."

"But if you muff this detail"—the general arose, dismissing Barrow—"you'll spend the rest of your time in the Corps on the forgotten list back in the auditor's office. Now, get out of here and make a name for yourself, because if you don't make out, you're a washout. You got the word. Good luck."

After Major Barrow waddled out of the office, the general slumped back into his canvas chair. He looked up at his adjutant and shrugged his shoulders.

"Washington!" he blurted. "Sometimes I wonder if they take this war seriously."

"But him . . ." Colonel Ward said, nodding toward the spot where Barrow had stood. "Why did they send a character like him out here?"

"Because every colonel to whom the command might have gone had enough seniority or political connections to refuse the assignment," Burgermeister explained. "Barrow is not a relative of the commandant and, apparently, knows no congressmen. And, fortunately, all he knows about the First Parachute Battalion is what he read in *Life* magazine."

"But those paratroopers will tear him apart."

"Of course they will," Burgermeister confirmed. "But what can I do? I was merely sent out here to win a war, and right now I wouldn't give six-to-five either way on how that will come out."

"I still think I had the best idea," Ward pointed out.

"Merge that battalion into the other outfits. Lose it among the regiments of the division. Disband it."

"And I can think of three very good reasons why that is an extremely poor idea," Burgermeister said wearily, getting up to stare out the window at the busy Nouméa streets. "I want that unit for raids and actions behind enemy lines. It's a splendid fighting outfit."

"It was."

"And," Burgermeister went on, "it is unthinkable to merge those paratroopers into the other organizations. They'd corrupt the entire division."

"You have a point there."

"And finally," the general sighed, "the commanding officers of the regiments have made out applications for retirement on disability, which they will submit if a single paratrooper is transferred into their commands. The skipper of the Fifth Marines even has a wire prepared to send to the Secretary of the Navy if I station the paratroopers within a country mile of his regiment. He'll claim such an act to be detrimental to the best interests of the Naval service and a calculated attempt to subvert his outfit."

"Well," Colonel Ward said begrudgingly, "maybe that man, Barrow, will turn the trick."

"And maybe the Japs will all drop dead."

"We'd have a chance then." Ward brightened.

"But only in this particular theater," Burgermeister said glumly.

Harold Barrow pondered the things told him by the general. He felt that he was enjoying a fabulous streak of luck. On the threshold of his greatest opportunity, he stood to realize the fulfillment of all the hopes and dreams he had brought into the Marine Corps with him years ago, none of which had ever before come close to materializing. Campaign bars he had found elusive, and medals had not existed for him. But now the general had promised recognition and important duties. Glory was attainable.

As bright as the future was, the present was cause enough for elation. From a dusty desk far removed from the sights and sounds of organized warfare, he had been picked up and dropped right into the middle of one of the most exciting chapters of Marine Corps history. From a clerk in Washington, he had become a combat leader in the Pacific Theater of War. And not only was he a commanding officer of fighting Marines, he was skipper of the elite troops, battle-proven men who had literally draped themselves with glory and honor. He had read about these rugged paratroopers, dreamed of their daring, and now he was to stand at their head. An awesome and gratifying thought.

Barrow did not share the general's reservations regarding the parachutists. Burgermeister had implied that his duties would be hard and tough, a challenge. The major, informed on the magnificent history of the paratroopers, was sure that his duties would be pleasant and rewarding. Any troops that had demonstrated such ability must have a vast reservoir of intelligence and courage. Barrow would cultivate those assets. He would win that fitness report, and the men back in the auditor's office would certainly take notice of their old fellow worker. He could see the look in their eyes when he went back to visit them with his five rows of campaign bars and medals, splashed with stars and clasps, a hero.

He determined to be a success. He would be tough and snap the men into line, a real Prussian. Or he would be kind and understanding and bring the men to him through affection. Like Napoleon, he would learn the name of every man in his battalion, share their aspirations and problems. Maybe he would give them a speech and lay it on the line as soon as he arrived in Tontouta: "Now hear this. This is the way it's going to be . . ." Or he would say nothing, watch everything, and keep them guessing.

Finally, he decided to wait and see just what the situation was before making definite plans. "I won't do a thing today except look around," he promised himself. "Tomorrow I'll know which way to move."

# 2.

Major Barrow made himself as comfortable as possible in the straight-backed seat of the jeep and drank in the exotic mountain scenery of New Caledonia as his driver guided the vehicle over the twisting highway on the ride to Tontouta, upisland from Nouméa. Following the contours of the Dumbea River, between the rugged New Caledonian Chaine Centrale, the jeep passed the side road leading to the Tontouta air strip; ahead lay a bridge, and to the left a group of pyramidal tents laid out in neat rows.

"There it is, the First Parachute Battalion," Barrow said, his eyes filling with pride. "My command."

The jeep driver glanced up at him and then swung his eyes back to the road. "In this outfit," he said sympathetically, "everybody gets a lousy break once in a while."

As the jeep swung into the area and stopped before the tents of the command section, Barrow surveyed his cherished realm of responsibility. The pyramidals stretched out in precise alignment, their rolled-up sides exposing immaculate interiors. The streets between the tents had been policed to perfection, and clean fresh sawdust had been spread under the Lister bags. The area was spick and span, a credit to the men who lived there and the officers who directed them.

Marines, dressed in clean khaki uniforms, scrubbed pith helmets and glistening paratrooper's boots, were engaged in working parties and guard mount, and the sound of troop and drill came from one of the company streets. A Marine with two prisoners in tow marched toward the river; and a company clerk, carrying a handful of reports, hurried into the first sergeant's tent. A typical Marine camp.

Major Barrow thought it odd that no one was on hand to greet him, since he had telephoned ahead, advising the battalion that their new commanding officer was on his way to Tontouta. He had hopefully supposed that would constitute an occasion. But he shrugged, thinking that maybe he had made better time than the trip from Nouméa usually took and was early in arriving. He walked toward the Officer of the Day's tent to check in.

"I'm Major Harold Barrow," he introduced himself to the captain who had the duty, "the new commanding officer of the battalion."

"Well, welcome to the outfit, Major," the captain said, snapping to attention. "I'm Captain Nugent of C Company. We heard you were coming but didn't really believe you'd show up."

"Why not?"

"Oh, we're always getting new commanding officers," Nugent explained vaguely, "but they generally chicken out and go over the hill before they get here."

Barrow examined the company commander as though trying to detect in the captain's appearance an indication of why he had uttered such a stupid statement. The captain's face and bearing told him little. Nugent's soft drawl suggested that he was from the Deep South, and his relaxed attitude and slow movements as he offered the major a handshake and a chair pretty much confirmed that impression. But he was friendly enough and made Barrow feel genuinely welcome.

"Sometimes it's kind of nice around here," Nugent volunteered, indicating the area with a sweep of his hand. "Once in a while someone shows up who actually likes it."

This remark, like his first one, was delivered in an obviously informal, offhand manner. It was, it seemed to Barrow, as though Nugent supposed the commander would stay only a short time and their acquaintance would be brief and casual.

"This is a fine-looking area," Barrow said, at least taking his own arrival for granted. "It indicates a high morale. The place is spotless."

"Yes, sir. It sure is," Nugent agreed proudly. "The men hire a gang of Kanaka natives to come in twice a week and police it up."

"Oh." Somehow Barrow was disappointed in that explanation of the area's immaculate condition. "Well, to whom shall I report. I might as well get down to business."

"Are you really going to stay?" Captain Nugent asked hopefully, almost eagerly.

"I have been assigned here by the commandant of the Corps," Barrow said impatiently. "Certainly I am going to stay."

"How long, sir?"

"Until I am properly relieved of my command."

"Imagine that!"

"To whom shall I report, please."

"Well, I've been acting as adjutant part time," the captain explained. "First Sergeant Maxwellington has been doing the paper work for the battalion. There's no one for you to relieve and Maxwellington can check you in on the paper routine at your leisure."

"Fine. Suppose you introduce me to First Sergeant Maxwellington."

"I'd be right proud to, Major."

As the two men walked into the dazzling tropical sunshine, Barrow's jeep driver came to attention and offered a salute.

"Your gear, sir?" he said.

Nugent looked toward the major. "You're really going to stay, sir?"

"Of course I'm going to stay," Barrow said, now actively annoyed because the tone of the captain's voice still implied that he expected the major to take off any minute.

"Put the major's gear in the first tent in officers' country," Nugent said, the delight in his voice apparent. "Right around the corner." He then led the new commanding officer into an adjoining tent.

"This is our new skipper, Major Barrow, First Sergeant Maxwellington," the Officer of the Day introduced Barrow to the Top Kick.

"Welcome, Major," Maxwellington said, looking Barrow over critically. "Hope you stay awhile."

"Thank you very much. I intend to," Barrow acknowledged the greeting. "At your convenience I'd like the up-to-date report on the battalion, including the roster, First Sergeant."

"Yes, sir," Maxwellington answered with more animation. "It will take me a few minutes to gather them up. Shall I deliver them to your tent?"

"That would be fine," Barrow said. "It will give me time to see a little of the area and unpack."

The tall, red-haired, raw-boned Scotsman began to hum happily as he opened his files and accumulated reports. He seemed convinced that Barrow might stay awhile.

Back in the company streets, Barrow's jeep driver was standing in front of the Officer of the Day's tent.

"Excuse me, sir," he said to Nugent. "May I use your telephone?"

"Why?" Nugent asked.

"Well, sir," the driver said sheepishly, "my jeep seems to be missing. I think it has been stolen. I'd like to call to Nouméa for another one."

"Go right ahead," Nugent said. "Help yourself." He led Major Barrow toward the company sections of the camp.

As they walked down the streets, Barrow was again thrilled by the splendid appearance of the battalion area and the industriousness of the paratroopers. However, he was not particularly pleased by some of the signs that hung over the tent entrances, announcing that they were the "Hotel Ritz," "Pink House" (named after a notorious institution outside Nouméa where men who weren't particular as to companionship were entertained), and such slogans as "Betty Grable Slept Here—We Wish" and "The Fastest Men in the World Pass Through These Portals." The major winced as he read some of the legends.

"These tents remind me of art galleries," Barrow said to the captain. "I never saw so many pin-up pictures.

The men certainly do admire Kathy Kennedy, don't they?"

"Yes, sir. They took a vote and decided she was what they are fighting for. Every man has at least one picture of the actress."

"I can understand that." Barrow grinned. "She surely is worth fighting for. But some of those French pin-ups are pretty objectionable. They don't look very nice, posted in the tents of the men."

"Well—" Captain Nugent considered the major's statement. "I wouldn't want to see them pinned up in tents of the officers."

In one of the tents, which bore a sign reading, "With the Help of God and a Few Marines, MacArthur Returns to the Philippines," Barrow observed a large group of Marines sitting at the feet of a first sergeant, listening intently to the lecture he was delivering.

"School?" he asked Nugent.

"Yes, sir," Nugent replied. "I guess you could call it that."

"Are classes held often?"

"Every day, sir."

"That's wonderful. The men do take this period of re-training seriously."

"They take everything seriously, Major."

In another tent, Major Barrow saw several men working on bolts of cloth, busily cutting and sewing.

"Parachuting is a hazardous occupation," he observed. "I suppose the parachutes demand constant attention and repair."

"I reckon so," Nugent answered, glancing into the tent and hurrying on.

At the end of a company street, toward the Dumbea

River, Barrow pointed to a Quonset hut that had part of one side blown off. "What happened to the Quonset, Captain?"

"Explosion."

"Obviously. What kind of an explosion?"

"TNT."

"How did the TNT come to explode?" Barrow was a little exasperated, not quite sure if Nugent was being deliberately evasive or failed to understand what he was trying to determine.

"Well, Major," Nugent explained, "you put a number eight tetryl cap into a block after crimping a length of instantaneous fuse into the primer . . ."

"I am trying to find out, Captain Nugent," Barrow interrupted, "if anyone was injured."

"No one was injured."

"Good. I suppose the explosion was accidental."

"Well, no, sir. It wasn't."

"Exactly what happened?"

"I don't rightly know, sir," Nugent answered. "First Sergeant Maxwellington decided to give the men a lecture on abstinence the other day, and while he was discussing the evils of drink, a couple of men set a satch charge off against the Quonset. Then they stole all the officers' whiskey and looted what was left of the chaplain's sacramental wine. The officers are furious."

"I don't wonder. Why didn't you post a guard on the Quonset?" the major demanded.

"I did. Naturally I did," the captain protested. "The corporal of the guard was sitting no more than three tents away from the Quonset playing poker when the TNT went off."

"Did he see anyone near the hut?"

"No, sir. He says he didn't even hear the blast."

"How closely did you question him?" the major asked.

"Well, not too closely," the captain admitted. "He's been drunk ever since. Hard to understand him."

The major let that startling statement go by, then asked, "How come he was playing poker while he was corporal of the guard?" He thought that was a reasonable question.

The captain thought the question over for a moment. "Well, he's a good poker player. I guess he *likes* to play poker. When he's winning, he's generally good for a five-dollar touch."

"Captain Nugent," Barrow said angrily, "do you realize how serious this is?"

"Yes, sir," the captain conceded, at the same time trying to soothe the upset major, "but it's not that serious. The officers can get some more whiskey."

"That's not what I mean," Barrow said, confounded by Nugent's attitude. "Government property has been destroyed, TNT has been expended without authorization and the crime of burglary has been committed."

"I never thought of it like that."

"You'd better have the corporal of the guard report to me in the morning," Barrow ordered. "We'll see if we can't get to the bottom of this."

"Very well, sir."

With this unpleasant revelation behind him, Barrow turned his interest back to the casual inspection of the area and the men he was to live among.

In C Company's area, Nugent and Barrow paused in front of a tent where a group of Marines were sitting on their bunks, singing and batting the breeze.

"Those men are off duty, I presume," Barrow said.

"Yes, sir. It's their cocktail hour."

"That's unusual. I never heard of such a thing."

"They picked the idea up from the New Zealanders while we were in Wellington," Nugent said. "But they can't stand tea so they substituted alcohol and grapefruit juice. Stump Juice cocktails. Shall we join them?"

"I don't think so . . ." Barrow began. "Officers don't generally . . ."

"They won't mind," Nugent assured the major. "They're very democratic."

Barrow followed Nugent, who had entered the tent. The host, Corporal Crocker, nodded toward the end of a bunk, inviting the officers to be seated. Corporal Martin and Pfc. Howes raised their hands in a "Hi," while Sergeant Fogleman made the officers feel at home by directing a wink toward them. Private Lincoln frowned at the two men and then resumed studying his cocktail.

"This is Major Barrow," Captain Nugent said simply.

"Hello, Major," the men said politely.

"I'm the new commanding officer of this battalion," Barrow added, somewhat sternly, appreciating the democratic attitude of the men but displeased by the informality which practically amounted to insubordination.

"That's okay," Pfc. Howes consoled him. "These wars don't last forever."

Corporal Crocker poured two canteen cups of Stump Juice for the major and the captain and served his guests. "This will make you forget your troubles," the corporal promised Barrow.

The major sipped his cocktail and studied his men while he listened to their chatter. He was a little dismayed by some of their conversation.

Pfc. Howes was arguing, "I'll bet the Japs do win this

war. Look at the way they held us off at Tanambogo. And they gave us a real bad time on Gavutu."

"We took both islands," Corporal Martin reminded him.

"Not until the 484 came in and blasted them off the hill on Tanambogo," Howes said smugly. "We could never have taken that island if it wasn't for the U.S.S. *Buchanan*."

"We took Gavutu with rifles and bayonets," Fogleman put in. "The 484 shelled only Tanambogo."

"Same difference," Howes insisted. "They were twin islands and the same battle."

"How many Japs were on the islands?" Barrow inquired. He had heard of this famous Gavutu-Tanambogo battle.

"About thirteen hundred," Howes said, as though that cinched his argument.

"And how many paratroopers hit the beach?" Barrow probed.

"Four hundred and eighty."

"Don't you think we did pretty well?"

"We did okay," Howes conceded, "but there's millions of Japs."

"And there's millions of us."

"Ah," Howes exclaimed in triumph, "but most of our men are in the Army or the Navy."

Private Lincoln looked up from his cocktail. "I don't see what difference it makes who wins the war," he said gloomily.

Barrow gave up. He sat quietly, listening to the talk and intently appraising these men of his, these men whose past conduct so belied their present utterances. Pfc. Howes, who minimized the heroic offensives of the

Solomons, had been one of the most determined warriors during the campaign. The major could easily imagine this Marine, of medium height and underweight, bolstering the firing line and then leading new advances with his blazing Johnson light machine gun. Recognized by the government through the award of a high decoration for outstanding conduct in combat and, even more important, acknowledged by his comrades as a top-caliber fighting man, the thin private first class decried his own efforts and those of his brave companions.

"Regardless of what he says," Barrow thought, "he is one good reason why the Japs cannot win this war."

Corporal Martin sounded as though the giant international conflict was merely a lark: he was going along with the Allied cause, not because he was devoted to the beliefs and way of life it was fighting for, but because he found war fun. The winning of fierce battles held no thrill for him comparable to that of landing on the shores of a friendly nation where whole new populations of girls offered him more challenge and greater rewards than the total defeat of an enemy brigade. Fat and happy, Corporal Martin put up with the unpleasantness of hostile contact with an organized enemy because he knew that, after the battle, he would be restationed on another island where the wine would flow and the women would smile.

Corporal Crocker seemed to feel that war was a profitable business. No matter where a man might find himself and no matter how austere the circumstances, a smart man could always turn a buck, Crocker believed. And war posed some wonderful opportunities. Vast quantities of the wealth of the United States were available to him to steal and then sell to some gullible customer. And war also brought equally wonderful shortages for him to fill. So, between campaigns, he happily distilled aniseed for thirsty sailors, hired entire Naval Construction Battalions to manufacture phony samurai swords and Japanese bayonets, and made himself a killing. His buddies admired him. He not only emphatically won every battle in his unique war, but when rifles spoke and machine guns chattered, Corporal Crocker could always be counted on to do more than his share to win the fighting battles—and, of infinite importance, he could generally produce a jug of anisette or a tin of medical alcohol even on the lines of resistance. A small man, hardly over five feet tall, he was a Goliath of accomplishment.

Sergeant Fogleman was a professional soldier; he accepted the periods of action and inaction as one and the same. Life was divided into two neat compartments: Marines were either in battle or preparing for battle. So it was a life of fight and retrain. A conscientious foot soldier, he was not concerned with the underlying causes of war. He trained well and fought well. It was a job. One thing above all else was to be remembered, and that wasn't brass bands, war bonds or waving flags: when the lead flies, keep your fanny down. And that, Fogleman always did, even when lugging sixty-millimeter mortar tubes or demolition kits through machine-gun fire as he applied his training and followed his trade.

Private Abraham Lincoln made Major Barrow nervous. The gaunt hillbilly, named after a more gentle man, must have joined the Marine Corps for one weird purpose. He was devoutly antisocial. When the First Parachute Battalion was called into action, he found a superb outlet for his meanness. Even so, the government found this "to be in keeping with the highest traditions of the United States Naval Service," and generously draped the Para-Marine with decorations.

Major Barrow saw Corporal Crocker reach under the blanket that hung over the cot he was sitting on and bring out a box of cigars, which he passed around. The major noticed the neat rows of five-gallon tins of medical alcohol, the boxes of cigars and cigarettes and candy piled under the cot.

"Where did all this gear come from?" he whispered to Captain Nugent. "Was it all expended?"

"War is a very wasteful business," Nugent said sorrowfully.

"It certainly is," Barrow gasped.

He found his cocktail very refreshing, but it was awfully strong stuff, he was thinking, because every once in a while it seemed to him that the seabag in the next tent moved. It appeared to be breathing. Finally he could stand the plaguing sight no longer; after shaking his head several times to try to rid himself of the persistent image, he excused himself and walked to the tent where the seabag leaned against the center pole. It was the domicile of the morale officer's assistant, Private Polk.

"What's in that bag, soldier?" he demanded.

"Dirty clothes, sir."

"Open it."

The morale officer's assistant opened the seabag and an obviously scared little Javanese woman tumbled out. She was naked.

"Now how do you suppose she got in there?" The assistant was very shocked. "If I find the guy who did this, I'll kill him. I'll report him to the Secretary of the Navy."

"Stop the act and tell me where she came from," Barrow commanded.

"She's an orphan, sir," Polk confessed, eying the pretty nude sorrowfully. "I put her in the seabag until I could accumulate some clothes for her. Can't let her run around like that."

"That's commendable, I suppose," Barrow said. "How long have you had to keep her hidden in that seabag?"

"About ten days, sir."

"Get her over to the quartermaster's shack and rustle her up some clothes," Barrow said in sudden fury, "and then get her out of this area."

"The poor kid . . ." Private Polk almost sobbed as he studied her beautiful lines. "The battalion was thinking of adopting her. She's only twenty."

"Where is the morale officer?" Barrow asked angrily. "I think he's going to have a new assistant."

"We lost him on Guadalcanal, sir."

"Oh." Barrow's anger abated. "That's too bad."

"Yes," Polk agreed. "He deserted, and we think he threw in with the Japs."

Barrow's anger returned in a flash. "If we have no morale officer," he blurted, "how come you're his assistant?"

The private scratched his head. "Would you repeat that question, sir. I don't think I understood it."

"In the absence of a morale officer," Barrow persisted, "what are your duties?"

"Oh"—the assistant brightened—"I drag the crap games for the company fund and issue beer chits. Morale is very high."

"Get that woman out of here," the frustrated major

shouted. "And I'll see if I can't find something more profound to occupy your time."

"Yes, sir."

The Officer of the Day and the men in the adjoining tent had not seen the incident—to all outward appearances—and were busy writing new verses to the "Marine's Hymn" when Major Barrow rejoined them.

The captain was adjudged the best lyricist when he came up with a new and original verse, which one of the men promptly copied down to send to *Leatherneck*, the Corps publication.

Captain Nugent sang, to the delight of the men:

> *"If you have a buddy, good and true,*
> *Clobber him before he clobbers you."*

"Ah, that's sweet," Private Lincoln sighed.

"Yeah," Pfc. Howes said. "Better than those corny old verses about Montezuma and Tripoli."

"Correct," said Corporal Martin. "That stuff was for the old Marine Corps. We ought to have a new hymn about Guadalcanal and Wake Island."

"If you have completed your philosophic serenade," Barrow said to the Officer of the Day, "let's get out of here." At the entrance to the tent he paused to thank the host for the drink. "It was very good," he said truthfully.

"Stop in any time, Major," Corporal Crocker acknowledged Barrow's thanks.

"They're well supplied with alcohol," Barrow observed to Nugent. "There must be quite a surplus of it."

"There always seems to be enough," Nugent recalled.

Near the Officer of the Day's tent, Barrow was surprised to see the jeep driver who had brought him to Tontouta still in the area. He was with another Marine from the motor pool.

"Why are you hanging around here?" Barrow asked.

"Well, sir," the driver explained, "I called Nouméa for another jeep and they sent Frank, here, to pick me up. I was over in the mess tent having a cup of coffee when Frank arrived."

"So?"

"Well, Frank came over to the mess tent to get me and he had a cup of coffee, too. When we got back here, it seems that Frank's jeep was missing, too. We think it's been stolen. Nouméa ain't got no more jeeps, so we're waiting to hitch a ride back to town."

"That's very odd," Barrow told Nugent as they walked toward his tent in officers' country. "Those men lose jeeps as though they were pins."

"Yes, sir," Nugent agreed. "Very irresponsible, those motor-pool men."

Barrow retired to his tent, unpacked his personal effects and stowed them in his foot locker, and then prepared to study the reports and orders which First Sergeant Maxwellington had left on his bunk. He had no more than sat down when there was a knock on the wooden posts that formed the tent doorway.

"Yes?"

"Can we see you a minute, Major?" It was Corporal Martin, accompanied by Pfc. Howes.

"Come in, men."

While Howes stood to one side, Martin extended an object toward Major Barrow.

"The men want you to have this, sir."

Barrow accepted the present. "Why, this is a Japanese

battle flag," he exclaimed as he unfolded the triangle of cloth and studied the Oriental characters on the flag, which was stained with dirt and brown spots that looked like dried blood. "It's very thoughtful of you to want to give this to me."

"Yes, sir," Martin said. "It's a genuine Jap banner. It flew from the top of the hill on Gavutu. It took us three days to get it. Had to crawl over a pile of our own dead to take the hill."

Barrow tried to imagine the scene. Battle-weary Marines, slashing and stabbing with their bayonets to conquer each contested inch of hill, men crumpling under the hail of deadly fire directed at them by Japanese who would die before they surrendered, the bodies of their own dead comrades the Marines had to tread on to accomplish their frightful mission.

"I'm deeply touched and most grateful." Barrow choked. "I'll treasure this as long as I live."

"Howes has got something for you, too," Martin went on, apparently satisfied with the major's reaction to the bloody gift.

"We thought you might enjoy this while you're off duty, sir," Howes said, bringing a case of bottled Stump Juice into the major's tent. "It's the greatest invention since the wheel."

"This is a most welcome gift." Barrow beamed. "I am very pleased. Tell the men how much I appreciate their thoughtfulness."

"Sure, Major."

After the two Marines left, Barrow held the soiled banner in his hands and gazed at the present of Stump Juice. "General Burgermeister must have this outfit mixed up with some other one," he mused. "These men are the finest ever assembled into one battalion in the whole Corps."

He put his gifts aside and picked up the official papers beside him. He examined the reports and orders of the day and then flipped to a communiqué headed:

> *To:* The Commanding General
> *From:* C.O., 1st ParaBn.
> *Subject:* Decorations and awards . . .

Barrow let his eyes drift down the impressively long list of men who had distinguished themselves in action against their country's enemies. He glanced again toward his Japanese battle flag, the proof of their heroism, and his eyes filled with tears.

# 3.

Early the next morning, Barrow breathed deep of the air blowing across the Chaine Centrale, which looked down on the camp, stretched luxuriously, then walked from officers' country to the command section of the paratroopers' camp to watch the daybreak activity of the men. He stood on the boardwalk that ran the length of the command section, into which the company streets entered, and was slightly annoyed to see that all the parachutists were still asleep in their pyramidals. There was no watch on the brig, and in the Officer of the Day's tent, a cot had been set up on which Captain Nugent was stretched out under the mosquito net. No guards were apparent in the area.

The major looked at his watch and frowned, and then walked along the boardwalk and stopped in front of the tent that was to be his office. He ran his hand lovingly over the red and gold sign which read "Commanding Officer," entered the tent and tried the chair in front of his desk. He was pleased.

Glancing again at his watch, Barrow left his office, walked back to the Officer of the Day's tent and stood at the end of the bunk.

"Captain Nugent," he said loudly. "Captain Nugent."

Captain Nugent grunted.

"Captain Nugent. Get up."

"What's the matter?" Nugent mumbled.

"There hasn't been any reveille yet."

Nugent peered at his watch and groaned. "It isn't even nine o'clock."

"What time do you generally hold reveille?" Barrow demanded.

"We haven't had a reveille since we left North Carolina," Nugent whined, protesting his early awakening.

Barrow was shocked. "No reveilles?"

"Yes, no reveilles."

"That's unheard of," Barrow exploded. "Every unit in the whole Marine Corps starts the day off with a reveille."

"Why?"

"Why! Because they do. Now suppose you get up and break out the noncoms for a reveille."

"They'll kill me," Nugent complained. "They'll think I'm drunk or crazy."

"That is an order, Captain," Barrow said emphatically.

"Yes, sir." The captain responded to the direct order with alacrity.

While Nugent went to wake up the noncoms of the battalion, Major Barrow returned to his office to prepare his schedule for the day. He was unable to think because of the screams of anguish that were coming from the tent rows. He listened in disgust.

"A reveille in the middle of the night," a man was lamenting. "We played poker until three o'clock this morning."

"He's trying to drive us over the hill," the voice of Corporal Martin rose above the other wails. "Don't he know there's a war on?"

"Fall out. Everybody out," the noncoms snarled. "Reveille."

One half-awake Marine dashed out into the company street with his rifle and bayonet. "Where are they?" he cried in alarm.

"Reveille, yard bird," a sergeant informed him.

"Reveille? What's that?"

"Are you trying to drive this outfit into a mutiny?" a private lashed at his sergeant. "Compared to you, a Jap looks good."

One drowsy private called to another, "Maybe the war is over and they're going to send us back to the States."

"If the war is over," Pfc. Howes was heard to say, "we lost it, because this certainly is a Jap trick."

Barrow's disappointment in the attitude of the paratroopers turned to anger, and he marched toward the men, who were forming lines in the streets for a roll call, to tell them that a simple reveille was no cause for the fantastic production they were making of it.

The cold stare he directed at the troopers softened as he viewed their depleted ranks. In some squads there were eight men, in others only two. Some platoons were reduced to a dozen men, where once had stood more than three times that number. In A Company he saw a one-man squad. The impact of this dramatic revelation of the decimation of his troops saddened the major, and he found he could not deliver the stern words he had planned. Instead he turned to waken the officers, who had not yet appeared.

"It's five minutes past nine, gentlemen," he announced as he entered their quarters.

The officers opened one eye each to stare at him in silent reprimand, then rolled over to go back to sleep.

"It's time you were about your duties."

"Yes, sir," the officers mumbled, hiding their heads under their pillows. "Right away, sir."

In his tent, First Sergeant Maxwellington watched the paratroopers stagger toward the Dumbea River, grumbling, to wash up and get ready for breakfast. He grinned happily.

"They never knew what hit them," he chortled to Major Barrow, who passed the tent on his way to the office. "It was just like the old Marine Corps."

"What was?"

"That good old-fashioned reveille you pulled on the men." The Top smiled. "Just like before we became nation-savers and prima donnas."

"I don't see anything unusual about a reveille." Barrow was upset by the implication in Maxwellington's words.

"Just like the old Marine Corps." Maxwellington was elated.

"As is done in every unit in the Corps," Barrow said to himself as he entered his own office. "You'd think I just pulled the second battle of Coral Sea."

The major straightened out the papers on his desk and officially began his first full day as Commanding Officer, First Parachute Battalion, First Marine Division, U.S.M.C. The turning point in his career had started and he was already well on his way toward eligibility for the Asiatic-Pacific campaign badge. He was now an integral part of World War II.

Now that the skipper was ready for office hours, Captain Nugent appeared at the doorway of the tent with the first order of business.

"I have Corporal Crocker here, sir," he announced. "He had the duty when the Quonset hut was blown up and the officers' whiskey stolen. You wanted to see him this morning."

"Show him in."

Nugent waved the corporal into the office, where he stood at attention before the major's desk.

Barrow studied the Marine, who beamed broadly on him, apparently not aware of the enormity of the offense he was to answer to.

"This is a very serious matter, Corporal Crocker."

"Yes, sir," Crocker agreed.

"And it appears to me that it was done with your knowledge and consent," Barrow went on. "Even with your participation."

"Oh, no, sir!" Crocker denied the crime with an air of aggrieved innocence.

"You were observed in a drunken condition after the whiskey was stolen," Barrow pointed out ominously.

"I had a few Stump Juice cocktails from the company supply," Crocker confessed.

"Oh. Well, it doesn't seem to me," the major continued, regaining his assuredness, "that you could have been only a few tents away from the explosion without having heard it."

"What, sir?" Crocker asked, turning one of his ears toward the major.

Barrow raised his voice. "I said it is impossible that you could have been so near the explosion without hearing it."

"I beg your pardon, sir," Crocker said, distorting his face in an effort to hear better. "A bomb went off near my head on Guadalcanal and it left me a little deaf."

"Suppose we take the Marine over to sickbay and have a corpsman give him a hearing test?" Barrow said to Nugent, angered by Crocker's brazen lie. "We'll find out just how deaf he is."

"Well," Nugent said undecidedly, "if you say so . . ."

"Why not?" Barrow snapped.

"What good would it do?" Nugent tried to explain. "He'd only look at the corpsman and say, 'What? What? What?' The doctor would have to admit him to the hospital and the hospital would transfer him to the States. He'd end up by getting a pension."

"What did you say, sir?" Crocker smiled brightly in the direction of the captain.

"Relieve this man of further duty as corporal of the guard until his hearing improves," Barrow said, surrendering to Nugent. To the corporal he whispered, "That is all."

"Thank you, sir," the happy corporal said, pleased that he had been relieved of the unpleasant duty.

As Crocker left the office, Barrow turned to Captain Nugent and, pointing toward the O.D.'s brassard on his arm, asked, "Why haven't you been relieved as Officer of the Day yet?"

"I've got the duty again today," Nugent answered.

"But you were O.D. yesterday. You shouldn't have the duty two days in a row."

"I lost," Nugent said.

"Lost?"

"We flip coins," Nugent explained. "I was odd man."

"And that's how we get our Officers of the Day?" Barrow asked in disbelief. "Well, that practice has got to halt immediately. I'll have a roster made out so the officers can share the duty."

"I don't think that's a very good idea, sir," Nugent said thoughtfully. "The officers will think you're persecuting them."

"I don't see why," Barrow said, surprised. "I think it's only fair to split the duty."

"We only have seven officers," Nugent explained. "We're fifty percent under strength. If you make out a roster, it means that we'll have to stand a watch once a week."

"All the more reason to take turns," Barrow said patiently. "Look at your case. You've had twenty-four-hour duty two days in a row."

"Yes, sir," Nugent conceded, "but generally, I'm pretty lucky. Yesterday was the first time I had the duty in three months."

"The matter is closed," Barrow said with finality. "I shall make out a duty roster."

As Captain Nugent hurried out to tell the junior officers the bad news, First Sergeant Maxwellington entered the tent and handed a communiqué to Major Barrow.

"This just came in from Nouméa," Maxwellington said, indicating the note he had placed on Barrow's desk. "I don't know how to answer it."

Barrow read the communication and then looked up at Maxwellington, confused. "This is from the motor pool. They request the use of six jeeps and a recon truck. It doesn't make sense."

"It would if you knew the men of this outfit," Maxwellington told him. "This is the only battalion in military history where every private has his own jeep, and a lot of them have recon trucks. Out in the woods, behind the camp, there's at least three ten-tonners."

"Where did they get them?"

"Well," Maxwellington skirted the question, "they weren't issued to them. The men would tell you they found them."

Barrow was troubled. "What do they use them for?"

"They court Navy nurses and go hell-raising in the jeeps," the Top disclosed, "and use the heavy jobs for bootlegging and smuggling. Nouméa is tracking down a rumor that they're running guns to the Japs."

The major grinned. "That's a good one."

"I don't disbelieve it," Maxwellington said sourly.

"Well, I do."

"Yes, sir. What are you going to do about the request from the motor pool?"

"The only thing I can do. Reject it," Barrow said. "As commanding officer, I can't accept this and, in so doing, admit that I know my men to be thieves. Write back to the motor pool and tell them I am insulted by their communiqué."

"That makes sense."

"And then we'll shake down the woods and recover the stolen equipment and have it returned."

"Don't get your hopes up, sir," the dour sergeant cautioned. "The men are experts at camouflage. The First Guard Company and all Army's M.P.s combed those woods and couldn't even find an oil stain."

"We'll try again," Barrow said determinedly, "and we'll find them."

"I can't share your optimism," the first sergeant said as he reached over to answer the telephone, "but I admire your spirit."

Maxwellington identified himself to the voice on the other end of the telephone and then handed the receiver to Major Barrow.

"It's Nouméa," the Top said. "The Officer of the Day in command headquarters says the call is for you."

Barrow took the phone and listened, dazed, to the voice from Nouméa, then gently put the instrument back on its cradle.

"Who was it?" asked the Top.

"General Burgermeister."

"What does he want?"

"It's about Private First Class Checkoway. I'm not sure I got it all quite straight."

"You probably did," Maxwellington assured him. "What has Checkoway done?"

"It seems he stole a plane over on the Tontouta strip and flew it, without a compass, all the way to Henderson Field on Guadalcanal. When he got to Guadal he gave them some fast talk and they tanked him up. Then he flew the F4U up to Rabaul and made three passes over the emplacements, strafing. The plane was rigged with a camera. It's the first time we've been able to get anything within a thousand miles of that place. It's the strongest Jap position south of the Home Islands." The major was out of breath just from thinking about that trip.

"Checkoway okay?"

"Believe it or not, yes. The general says that if the man has a good service record, he's going to write him up for a Congressional Medal of Honor. Otherwise, he goes to

Portsmouth Naval Prison. What kind of a record does he have?"

"Probably the best one in this battalion," Maxwellington said, "but that's not good enough. He'll go to Portsmouth. It must be nice in New Hampshire at this time of year, the lucky bum."

"That's a hell of an attitude for a first sergeant." Barrow arose angrily from his chair.

"That was a hell of a thing for a Pfc. to do," Maxwellington countered.

"True. But it's done," Barrow said. "I hope he gets a medal for his daring, but, in the meantime, we'll have to arraign him for a general court-martial for stealing the plane."

"According to what you just said," the Top pointed out, "General Burgermeister has taken it upon himself to write up either the citation or the specs for a court-martial."

"But Checkoway is attached to this battalion," Barrow protested. "As commanding officer, I should recommend the action to be taken in this case."

"That's a fact," Maxwellington agreed, "but it's academic now. General Burgermeister outranks you."

"Well," Barrow said indecisively, "confine Checkoway in the battalion brig as soon as he is delivered here."

"Yes, sir."

Captain Nugent entered the tent. His brow was furrowed with worry. "I wish you'd do something about Captain Butts and Lieutenant Chesley. They're not speaking to each other and their feud is depressing all the other officers."

"I'm sorry to hear that," Barrow said, aware that high morale among officers is a most important factor in an effective organization. "What happened between them?"

"Well, it was all Captain Butts' fault," Nugent said in heat. "He ought to be shot."

"What happened?" Barrow repeated.

"Chesley was making out but good with the most beautiful girl on New Caledonia," Nugent explained, "and you know how scarce girls are on this island. They were engaged. Anyway, Chesley was wining and dining her in the Hotel Metropole when Captain Butts joined them. During the evening, Chesley went to the head, and when he came back, both the girl and Butts were gone. When Chesley saw the girl the next day, she wouldn't speak to him except to use vile and abusive language. You know what Butts did?"

"Can't imagine."

"He told the girl that Chesley was a nice guy but that he was a rake and a philanderer. Said that Chesley had a wife in Los Angeles and another one in Wheatland, Wyoming. And Chesley ain't got no wife in Los Angeles. Now, what do you think of a guy like that? And Chesley had been buying the drinks."

"I guess Chesley has a case."

"You bet. Still," Nugent mused, "I'm not so sure but what Chesley does have a wife in Los Angeles, too."

"I thought the problem might be of a military nature," Barrow interrupted. "I doubt that their romances are of any concern to me."

"I reckon," Nugent sighed. "But wait until that girl finds out that Butts has a wife in Cincinnati and a paternity suit in St. Louis."

A Marine private, whom Major Barrow had not seen

in the area before, stood respectfully in the tent doorway and spoke to Captain Nugent.

"Hi, Captain," the private said. "Would you tell the company clerk to let me draw my back pay?"

"Hession," Nugent shouted, grabbing the man by the hand and shaking it vigorously. "Where have you been? We ain't seen you for months. We thought you stole a sailor suit and went back to the States on a battlewagon. You're listed as a deserter."

"I been to Auckland, New Zealand," Hession said, sitting on the edge of Barrow's desk as he spoke. "Went down for the first day of the summer meet and kind of liked it, so I stayed awhile. I got married while I was there."

The major, fascinated by the reception accorded the deserter, wanted to know how the prodigal son had gotten to New Zealand and back to New Caledonia.

Hession was an honest man. "A clerk down in command, in Nouméa, gave me a copy of rest and recreation furlough papers. The company clerk in C Company typed me out a set and I wrote in the three endorsements. I signed General Burgermeister's name—but only on one copy, which I destroyed in Auckland. Then I went aboard the M.S. *Cape Flattery* and gave the mate a copy of my papers and took passage on her to Auckland. To get back, I told the Navy disbursing officer in New Zealand that I was on furlough and had lost all my papers. He got me a seat on the Pan American clipper. Very cold, flying back here."

"You better lock him up, Captain," Barrow observed, "and hold him for a court-martial."

"I guess so," Nugent said reluctantly, "but you'll have

to help me write up the specifications. I wouldn't know exactly where to begin, what with New Caledonia being a French possession, New Zealand part of the British Empire, the *Cape Flattery* being part of the Merchant Marine, the PanAm being civilian, and Hession being a member of the Marine Corps. If he calls for witnesses, it will break the government."

"This girl I married," Hession offered helpfully, "her old man is a Member of the New Zealand House of Parliament. The Minister of Defense, or something like that."

Barrow had learned one thing during his years in the Marine Corps, and that was not to fight the problem. Realistically, he abandoned the planned court-martial.

"As Commanding Officer's punishment," he told Hession, "you are restricted to this area and awarded a hundred hours of extra police duty."

"My father-in-law will be disappointed," Hession said. "He and Admiral Dorsey were going to have me detached to Wellington, New Zealand, for consular duty. Washington already approved."

"We'll cross that bridge when we come to it," Barrow said in near desperation. "In the meantime, you're restricted to camp."

"Yes, sir."

Two Marine M.P.s, flanking a small man wearing paratrooper's boots, stepped aside in the tent doorway as Hession left Major Barrow's office.

"We've brought back Private Williams," they announced proudly to Captain Nugent and the commanding officer.

"Who is Private Williams and where has he been?"

Barrow demanded. "Don't tell me he's another deserter reporting in from New Zealand for his back pay."

"Oh, no, sir," the private assured the major as he and the two M.P.s entered the tent and stood near Nugent. "I've just been over in the Casual and Replacement Battalion, acting as first sergeant."

"How did you work that?" Captain Nugent asked in admiration. "You flunked all the tests for Pfc. back in New River."

"I heard they were short-handed for high-ranking enlisted men," Williams explained, "so I packed my seabag and reported there with top-kick stripes on my arm. I told them I was a first sergeant and that my service record book would be forwarded later. They believed me and made me a first sergeant of C Company—largest company in the Pacific."

"How did you get through the duties?" Barrow asked the brazen Marine.

"Easy," Williams said immodestly. "I appointed some sergeants and put them in charge of all working parties. Then I had two liberty passes made out for each man. One was always in my desk so that every man was always logged in, and the men carried the other one with them so that they were always on authorized liberty. See, that way a guy can never be over the hill. I ran off one hundred percent more beer chits than there were men so I'd never suffer a beer shortage. One can for each man, and I got one can for each man on the roster."

"That's all very interesting," Barrow said, "but what you're saying may be used against you at your court-martial. Captain Nugent will conduct you to the brig."

"I'm sorry, sir," one of the M.P.s said, embarrassed.

"What are you sorry about?" Barrow wanted to know.

"We only brought Williams up here to pick up his gear. We've got to return him to Casual and Replacements."

"I don't understand," Barrow said. "Why should he be confined in the C and D area?"

"He's not going to be confined, sir," the M.P. explained. "Private Williams did such a fine job as first sergeant that the colonel who commands C and D wants him back as his permanent top kick."

"If the colonel wants this man, he'll have to go through channels," Barrow snapped, "after the court-martial."

"Well," the M.P. said hesitatingly, "it seems that he's already done that. The colonel made a deal with General Burgermeister. They didn't want Williams locked up, so they transferred him to C and D and made his transfer retroactive as of six weeks ago."

"I can't believe the general would do a thing like that."

"All I know is the facts, sir," the M.P. pointed out. "I only brought Williams up here to pick up his gear and records."

"It's hard to understand General Burgermeister doing a thing like that," Barrow said bitterly. "A few such incidents and the whole Marine Corps will fall apart."

"Imagine!" Nugent beamed on Private Williams. "Five stripes in one promotion. That must set a record."

"Maybe I should have held out for sergeant major," Williams reflected as he reached into his pocket and took out several sets of first sergeant's stripes. "Will you return these to First Sergeant Maxwellington? Tell him I borrowed them."

"Sure," Nugent said.

Barrow shook his head in sad confusion. "Instead of going to the brig as he deserves, he receives a fantastic promotion. Organizations just aren't run that way."

"That's right, sir." Nugent, too, was impressed. "I suppose we should be very proud of Private Williams."

# 4.

The new commanding officer of the First Parachute Battalion was not at all reluctant to follow Captain Nugent's suggestion that they take a coffee break. He needed a pause to refresh himself and to organize his thoughts. He was not new to the Corps, but it had never occurred to him that flagrant violations of regulations would go unpunished—even be rewarded. Honest hard work and good soldiering, he had always understood, were the route to promotions and added responsibilities in the Marines. But in this battalion, it seemed, the shortest road to the greatest rewards was through the smashing of every rule in the book.

Of course he realized that the gross fakery of Crocker, the amazing exploit of Checkoway and the incongruous finales to the misdeeds of Hession and Williams were exceptional, just as it was a mere coincidence that he had been exposed to the awful series of high crimes and misdemeanors in such rapid-fire order. Well, probably it was best to get the unpleasant things behind him so that he could settle down to the enjoyable and wonderful experiences known only to combat leaders.

"Good morning, sirs." The cook smiled at the officers as they each drew a cup of coffee from his urn. "This is a happy day."

Barrow, assuming that this was the cook's way of welcoming him to the outfit, smiled back his pleasure.

"Why?" Nugent asked, spoiling the illusion. "It's just like yesterday."

"Oh, no, it isn't," the cook contradicted. "Masterson has extended me an invitation to attend his dance tonight."

"Well, lucky you," Nugent responded.

"Yeah." The cook was quite overwhelmed by his good fortune. "But it cost me. I had to give the quartermaster twenty bucks to fix breakfast."

"Can this quartermaster cook?" Barrow asked.

"No, sir."

"Then you can't allow him to cook breakfast for the men."

"I have already paid him," the cook insisted.

"Have you thought of the troops who must eat the quartermaster's cooking?" Barrow demanded.

"If the quartermaster is willing to give it a try," Nugent sided with the cook, "the men should be willing to go along. Besides, the quartermaster took the money."

"So?"

"So he must have confidence."

"I suppose."

Nugent finished his coffee and turned back to the cook. "On your way over to the strip, stop at C Company and pick up Masterson's mail for him."

"Okay, sir."

Barrow didn't like the situation but decided to concentrate his interests on the more important business of military training and discipline. He followed Nugent from the mess tent. "It's still not correct, though," he complained. "He should be thinking in terms of a menu and he's planning on an all-night dance."

"Masterson puts on some very fine dances, sir," Nugent assured the major. "Every off-duty nurse on the island will be there. You ought to try to get to know Masterson and maybe he'll invite you to one of them."

"That would be nice," Barrow said, "but what is his mail doing in this area?"

"He's one of our men," Nugent said. "He's a corporal in C Company."

"Why is he over on the Tontouta strip? Detached duty?"

"Not exactly, sir."

"Well, who sent him over there?"

"No one, sir. He went over by himself."

"Be specific. What is he doing at Tontouta and how long has he been there?"

"You might say he's over the hill, sir," Nugent said reluctantly. "He's been over there for two months."

"He's been over the hill for two months and you know where he is!" Barrow stammered in utter confusion. "Why haven't you had him brought back in?"

"It's not quite that easy, sir," Nugent hedged.

"What's so difficult about picking up a deserter?"

"Well, you see, sir, he's a colonel now. He's the commanding officer of the strip."

"He's a corporal in our C Company and he's a colonel at the strip, less than a mile from here!" Barrow's confusion mounted. "Who appointed him a colonel?"

"No one."

"Then how can he be a colonel?"

"He made himself a colonel, sir."

"You have lost me, Captain Nugent," Barrow said.

"You have completely lost me. How in the world can a Marine corporal promote himself to colonel?"

"Well," Nugent explained, as though it were all quite simple, "he set himself up a tent and found himself a pair of chicken colonel's insignia. He made himself commanding officer of the area."

"Just like that!" Barrow exploded. "A PX colonel. A character to amuse the aviators."

"They don't find him very amusing over at Tontouta, sir," Nugent defended the corporal. "I heard that he's had leaf colonels thrown into his brig, and he promotes and busts men left and right."

"Impersonating an officer!" Barrow exclaimed. "That's even worse than desertion. We'd better get him back here and lock him up before Nouméa hears about this. They'll hang him."

"Nouméa is aware of Masterson already," Nugent pointed out. "General Burgermeister gave him the Efficiency Award last month for running the best command on the island, and Masterson sits in on the general's staff meetings. He's Burgermeister's right-hand man."

"He was," Barrow said emphatically. "Call my jeep and we'll drive over to the strip and relieve Masterson of his command."

"If you insist, sir," Nugent cautioned. "But I'd go slow. I wouldn't want to tangle with Corporal Masterson while he's still a colonel. He might throw us both in his brig."

"Get a jeep."

"If you insist, sir . . ."

"I insist."

"Very well, sir. Shall I pick up Masterson's mail for him?"

"No. Don't you understand? We're going to bring Masterson back here."

Sitting beside Nugent on the short trip to the air strip, Barrow nervously tried to plan what he would tell the real commanding officer of the area. It was unpleasant business, and with Captain Nugent gaily humming beside him, he had difficulty forming the delicate words he would have to deliver.

"What's the name of the duly appointed commanding officer of the air strip, Captain?" he wanted to know.

"Major O'Connell," Nugent answered. "A real tough old soldier."

"Poor Masterson."

"Yeah," Nugent said, worried. "I hope this won't interfere with Masterson's dance tonight."

"Captain Nugent," Barrow said severely, "do you realize the enormity of this situation? The corporal has been over the hill long enough to be termed a deserter and, during time of war, could be shot for that offense. He has impersonated an officer and usurped a command. He has hoodwinked a general and has abused every privilege that goes with the high rank he has illegally assumed."

"That's pretty rough," Nugent said with concern. "We'll have to get someone else to put on the dances, I guess."

Captain Nugent brought the jeep to a halt in front of the Officer of the Day's office in the strip area. A lieutenant, wearing the O.D.'s arm brassard and a pistol, walked up and smartly saluted the major as he got out of the jeep.

"Where might I find Major O'Connell?" Barrow asked

the Officer of the Day after returning the lieutenant's salute. "I'd like to speak with him."

"Is it important that you speak with him, sir?" the lieutenant asked. "I think he'd rather you came around next week."

"It's very important, Lieutenant."

"Well, I'm not sure . . ."

"Is he at a meeting? Is he ill?" Barrow inquired.

"Not exactly, sir," the lieutenant answered.

"Well, why can't I see him?"

"He's not receiving many visitors, sir," the Officer of the Day said uneasily.

"Why not?"

"Well, sir, he's in the brig."

"The major? In the brig?"

"Yes, sir. Colonel Masterson had him flung in the brig for five days bread and water for insubordination. It seems that Major O'Connell put too much grapefruit juice in Colonel Masterson's alcohol . . ."

"Where is the brig?" Barrow interrupted.

"Over there behind those tents, sir"—the O.D. pointed —"but . . ."

"Thank you."

Barrow strode determinedly across the area to the brig for the unpleasant interview with Major O'Connell. He hoped he could get his corporal back to the paratroopers' camp before the major lowered the boom.

A Marine guard, his carbine slung over his shoulder, sat on the edge of a bunk in the brig, playing poker with the prisoners.

"I'd like to speak with Major O'Connell," Barrow said to the guard.

"I'm Major O'Connell," said one of the prisoners, squeezing off his cards. "What do you want?"

"I'd like to speak with you alone, Major," Barrow said.

Major O'Connell continued squeezing off his cards, peeking intently at each one as it slowly revealed itself. "Some other time," he told Barrow.

"It's very important that I speak to you right now, Major," Barrow insisted.

O'Connell very carefully put his cards face down on the bunk and covered them with half-dollars. He picked them up, peeked again at them, glanced around at his fellow prisoners, then put the cards in his shirt pocket and buttoned it. "I open for three bucks," he said, "and looking for a raise." He got up and stepped outside the tent with Major Barrow as the guard counted out three dollars to call the bet.

"Well?" O'Connell demanded of Barrow. "Make it quick."

"This is terrible," Barrow said, surveying the brig. "It's very embarrassing."

"Correct," O'Connell agreed impatiently. "Is that what you came to tell me?"

"No."

"Well, get on with it. Everybody called me and I got a raise. That's going to be the best pot of the day."

"This man, Masterson . . ." Barrow blurted. "He isn't a colonel at all. He's a corporal from my battalion, masquerading as an officer."

"What?" O'Connell roared. "Masterson is an impostor?"

"Yes, Major. You're still the real commanding officer here."

"And you're nothing but a troublemaker," O'Connell lashed at Barrow.

"But . . ."

"But nothing," O'Connell interrupted in fury. "Do you realize that I have been thrown into this brig three times? By a corporal! Do you want to make me the laughingstock of the whole Marine Corps?"

"Of course not."

"If the word ever got out that I did bread and water on the whim of a corporal, I'd never be able to hold my head up again," O'Connell hissed. "I'd have to retire."

"Well, something has got to be done about this situation."

"And I suppose you've heard that General Burgermeister has awarded Masterson the Efficiency plaque for having the best-run unit in New Caledonia?" O'Connell continued, ignoring Barrow's statement.

"I've heard that, too."

"And you are determined to make a fool of the general?" O'Connell demanded. "You insist on ruining the careers of two officers, one of them a general?"

"That wasn't my intention at all," Barrow protested. "I came over here to arrest Masterson."

"You're out of your head," O'Connell said through clenched teeth. "Burgermeister will slaughter you if you mess with Masterson."

"Well, something's got to be done."

"That's right," O'Connell confirmed. "I've got it all figured out. You just leave this area, never come back, and forget that you've ever been here."

"But, Major O'Connell . . ."

"Look," O'Connell snapped at Barrow, showing him

his cards, "a straight flush. This is the best hand I've had all day and those guys are into me for eighteen bucks. Now, will you please get out of here so I can get back to the game?"

"What about Masterson?"

"I'll tell you what about Masterson," O'Connell threatened. "If you ain't on your way in thirty seconds, I'll call him and we'll have you thrown into this brig, too."

"I guess you're not going to bring Masterson back after all," Nugent said as Barrow got back into his jeep. "Too bad we didn't bring his mail over with us."

"We're not going to bring Masterson back," Barrow admitted.

"That's good," Nugent said. "Masterson's a fine man."

Nugent's sigh of relief angered Barrow. "Your dance will be held as scheduled," he said sarcastically.

"Want me to see if I can get you an invitation?"

"Please don't bother. Maybe some other time."

On the trip back to the parachutists' camp, Nugent recalled some of Masterson's exploits in action. "On Gavutu," Nugent said, "that guy wiped out a cave containing the Japanese command. Probably cut down resistance by two days."

"That was commendable," Barrow conceded. "He must be a fine fighting man."

"When he has to be," Nugent said. "But on the day I'm telling you about, Masterson saw these six Jap officers go into a cave. We couldn't hold Masterson back. Boy, did he take off after those Nips!"

"He really hates Japs," Barrow said, his anger abating somewhat.

"No," Nugent said, dismissing that thought. "All six

officers were carrying beautiful samurai swords. The sailors pay more than a hundred dollars each for them."

Barrow stared grimly ahead for the remainder of the trip. Nugent, he found, gave him very little helpful information, but much disillusionment. He decided to speak to the captain only when necessary.

As they drove up before his office, Barrow, looking toward the Dumbea River, found it necessary to speak to the Officer of the Day.

"Captain Nugent," he said, pointing toward the river. "That's not right."

Nugent glanced toward the river, where prisoners and guards had congregated. "What isn't right, sir?"

"Captain Nugent," Barrow began patiently, "I realize that all these men are comrades—that they have gone through much together—but it is not right for the prisoners to hold machine guns while the guards go in swimming."

"Yes, sir," Nugent agreed with emphasis. "I told those men to take turns. I'll see that the prisoners have their time in the water, too."

"You're mixed up, Captain," Barrow said. "Prisoners should not be handling weapons under any consideration. It's not a question of taking turns. And the guards should not be taking a swim while they are guarding prisoners."

"Well, sir . . ."

"It's just a little thing that should be rectified," Barrow said, his voice stiffening. "Please correct the condition."

"If you insist, sir."

"Why should I have to insist?" Barrow demanded. "I merely state that it is not correct for prisoners to hold machine guns for the guards."

"But I promised the guards they could go swimming if they took the duty," Nugent explained.

"Do you have to bribe them to get them to perform their duties?" Barrow asked angrily.

"Well, sir," Nugent answered, "if I don't let them go swimming, they won't stand guard."

"Who's running this outfit," Barrow snarled, "the officers or the men?"

"Well," Nugent hedged, "I've got to be fair. The guards deserve a swim, too."

"Your logic is lost to me," Barrow said. "Let the guards take their swims when they get off watch."

"It's either too early or too late then."

"Let's not make a production of this, Captain," Barrow ordered. "Tell the guards to keep out of the water and hold onto their weapons."

"Very well, sir, if you insist."

"If I insist! Well, I insist."

"Yes, sir." Nugent gave up. "Only tomorrow there won't be any guards at all."

Barrow was shocked by that statement. "Why not?"

"Because all the men love to swim," Nugent explained. "If only the prisoners are allowed to go into the water during the day, the men will all get themselves thrown into the brig."

"This is ridiculous."

"I could take the ammunition away from the guards," Nugent offered as a solution. "Then the prisoners would have weapons without ammo. Would that be all right?"

"What good would it do to give the guards weapons if you don't issue them ammunition?"

"All right," Nugent conceded. "I'll take the weapons away from the guards."

"That is not the solution, either, Captain," Barrow said.

"Very well," Nugent said with enthusiasm. "I'll close the brig and make all the prisoners go back to full duty. It's about time we got some work out of them, anyway."

"No. Don't do that," Barrow groaned. "Just take the machine guns away from the prisoners."

Nugent's further protests were drowned out by the noise of a large truck that pulled into the area. As the two Marines watched, a tall civilian climbed out of the truck cab and approached them.

"Is Colonel Crocker in, sirs?" the French civilian asked.

The major didn't know whom the man was talking about. Corporal Crocker was the only man in the battalion with that name.

"I'll inquire," Captain Nugent told the Frenchman before Barrow could tell the visitor he was in the wrong area. "Whom shall I say is calling?"

"Jacques Pierre Valencourt. Please tell him I have come about the consignment of anisette."

Captain Nugent motioned Major Barrow to accompany him as he went to find "Colonel" Crocker. "This Valencourt is the richest trader on the island and a real political influence. How do you suppose Crocker could have gotten mixed up with him?"

"You're pretty sure the Frenchman wants to speak to our Crocker?" Barrow asked. "What would Crocker have to do with a consignment of anisette?"

"Oh, Crocker runs the battalion still," Nugent answered as they entered the tent where a group of men were drinking Stump Juice out of canteen cups. "He has a fine head for business."

"Another phony colonel," Barrow muttered as he followed Nugent.

"Have a drink?" the men greeted the two officers.

"No, thank you," Barrow said. He turned to the corporal he had come to find. "Colonel Crocker," he said sarcastically, "Jacques Pierre Valencourt is here to see about a consignment of anisette. Will you see him, sir?"

"Sure," Crocker said. "Tell him I'll be out as soon as I get dressed."

The major and the captain delivered the corporal's message, and a few minutes later Crocker joined them with full colonel's chickens on his shoulders. They clashed incongruously with the corporal's stripes on his arms.

"I'd like to increase my order by another hundred gallons," the Frenchman said after shaking hands with the paratrooper. "I have signed up the American officers' mess as well as the French government forces."

"Very well," the corporal-colonel agreed as he wrote down the order. "But I'll need another three days to run off the extra hundred gallons. I'll have to hire another dozen Javanese for the still."

"But I promised delivery tomorrow," Valencourt protested.

"I'm sorry," Crocker said with finality. "I committed all the anisette I have on hand to Admiral Dorsey. He's retailing it to his fleet. And I'll have to work my Javanese overtime as it is. You'll have to absorb the additional costs of overtime in the sales price."

The Frenchman was disappointed. "If that's the best you can do, I suppose I'll have to be content. I'll hold back some of the supply I was to deliver to the French army and make a partial delivery to the American officers' mess. It was a cash transaction."

Crocker nodded. "How about next week's order? Same amount?"

"Yes, plus another fifty gallons. Business is picking up at the Pink House now that the fleet is in."

As the visitor got back into his truck, he called to the corporal, "This truck is in just as good working order as you promised. I'm having very good luck with it."

Major Barrow looked at the truck more closely. It was obviously a G.I. vehicle. Through the thin coat of new paint he could read the lettering which indicated it had once been the property of H and S Company, Seventh Marines.

"Did you sell the Frenchman that truck?" Barrow demanded as the civilian drove out of camp.

"Yes, sir."

"It belongs to the Seventh Marines," Barrow pointed out. "You have no business selling the equipment of that regiment."

"Impossible," Crocker said, removing the eagles from his shoulders. "The Seventh Marines were stationed on Samoa before they landed on Guadalcanal. They've never been within a thousand miles of New Caledonia."

"He's right," Captain Nugent confirmed. "The Seventh Marines are still in the Solomons."

"That doesn't excuse the fact that the truck was probably stolen and never was Crocker's to sell," Barrow insisted.

"Well, if it didn't belong to the Seventh Marines," Nugent wanted to know, "who did it belong to?"

"It belonged to the United States government," Barrow said severely. "That's who it belonged to."

"Correction, sir," Crocker interrupted. "The government transferred its surplus equipment to the British administration in Apia before the Seventh Marines pulled out of Samoa for the Solomons."

"Then it belongs to the British government."

"All I know," Crocker said, losing patience with the major, "is that General Burgermeister asked me to make a truck available to Jacques Valencourt. He didn't have any trucks to give the Frenchman, so he paid half of the purchase price on the one I sold him."

Major Barrow was glad to see First Sergeant Maxwellington, who approached with a message from Nouméa. The major had yet to win his first argument as commanding officer, and he knew he could never stand up under the bold corporal's presentation of the facts as he knew them and Captain Nugent's weird logic.

"This is from the Naval Medical Headquarters," Maxwellington said, handing the communiqué to Barrow. "They've got a gripe. It seems that most of the sheets have been stolen from Mobile Hospitals Five and Seven. Even the nurses' quarters were looted of linen. The patients and nurses are sleeping on mattress covers. Burgermeister wants every command to help try to locate the sheets."

"I can't imagine why anyone would want to steal all those sheets," Barrow said, "but we'll post the communication and bring it to the attention of the men. They might have heard something about it."

"What about Crocker and the truck?" Nugent asked.

"I don't think I care to be involved in the situation," Barrow said. "If the general knows about it, let him assume responsibility. But if it is ever brought to my attention officially, I'll report the whole incident."

"To whom?"

"I don't know," Barrow admitted, walking toward the battalion bulletin board with First Sergeant Maxwellington. "I just don't know."

Major Barrow and First Sergeant Maxwellington stood aside to let a group of Marines march past. The guard was being changed. Barrow watched with pride as his men snappily executed the ceremonies of guard relief and the posting of new sentries, but was puzzled by the appearance of several Javanese and Kanakas in the ranks of the paratroopers.

"Why are those Oriental civilians marching with the Marines?" he wanted to know.

"Those are rifle bearers," Maxwellington answered.

"Rifle bearers?" Barrow's brow wrinkled into a confused frown. "Since when do Marine privates have servants to carry their rifles?"

Maxwellington shrugged. "Most of the privates have one. All of the machine gunners and BAR men have a boy to tote their weapons."

"I never saw anything like that," Barrow stammered.

"Neither have I," Maxwellington said. "It might be a good idea if it weren't against regulations."

"I think we had better put a stop to it."

"I agree." Maxwellington nodded his head. "We couldn't take the rifle bearers into action with us, anyway. The BAR men and machine gunners will scream when they have to carry their own pieces, but they'll get over it."

"That's nice to know."

Before he approached the bulletin board to pin up the notice from the Naval Medical command, Barrow stopped and looked toward the tent where classes were being held.

"That is the same first sergeant who was conducting school yesterday," he pointed out, "and it looks as though the same men are sitting in on the classes. Does one first sergeant hold all the schools? Don't other men attend them?"

"That first sergeant happens to be the only man in the battalion who passed the bar," Maxwellington explained. "He used to be a lawyer in Philadelphia."

"I don't get the connection."

"All those men you see in the tent," Maxwellington said, "are P.A.L.s—prisoners-at-large. The first sergeant is giving them a series of lectures on how to beat a court-martial. They all got courts coming up. He charges a buck a lecture, money back if the boys don't beat the raps. In the afternoon they have classes in Japanese."

"That's horrible." Barrow was shocked. "That's making a mockery of military justice."

"That ground has been covered," Maxwellington informed the major. "The first sergeant has permission from Nouméa to hold classes. Command ruled that the men are entitled to counsel."

"That's counsel?"

"By official decree," Maxwellington confirmed. "General Burgermeister was going to stop it, but the first sergeant threatened to bring suit against him for obstructing justice and depriving the men of their rights. The general took the easy out and said it was okay."

Barrow turned to the other reason classes were being held. "Why are they holding classes in Japanese?"

"In case we lose."

"In case we lose the war?" Barrow asked angrily.

"That's right."

"That's wrong. It smacks of treason. It's unthinkable that a Marine battalion could develop such an attitude. I'll stop that quick."

"You'll never get by General Burgermeister's Intelligence Section," Maxwellington cautioned the major. "They'll stop you like a ton of bricks."

"Why?"

"Intelligence doesn't care why the men are learning Japanese but they are anxious that they learn. There ain't more than three Marines in the whole Corps that speak that language, and Intelligence needs interpreters. The D-2 section of General Burgermeister's headquarters is underwriting the cost of the course and is supplying the texts."

"It seems to me," Barrow said, feeling frustration, "that the general and his staff take quite an interest in this battalion."

"No," Maxwellington corrected, "it's just that the general and his staff get involved once in a while."

"I think I now know," Barrow mused, "what General Burgermeister was trying to tell me yesterday."

The party was still going on in the tent where Barrow had been served Stump Juice cocktails the day before. Barrow listened to new verses of the "Marine's Hymn" as they filled the air.

> *"The Army takes the medals,*
> *And the Navy takes the queens,*
> *But the boys who take the reaming*
> *Are the United States Marines."*

"Those men have been writing new verses to the Hymn for two days," Barrow observed. "How come they have so much free time?"

"That's the Board of Directors," Maxwellington said sourly. "The battalion brain-trusters."

"It occurs to me," Barrow said, "that the officers of a battalion would constitute a logical Board of Directors for a Marine command."

"That would apply to the old Corps," Maxwellington said. "It's a new outfit now."

"What need do the men have for a Board of Directors?"

"I guess you haven't heard," Maxwellington said, "but this battalion is incorporated. They found some ancient legal decision, back in North Carolina, that applied to professional soldiers during the Revolution. They petitioned the state and received their charter of incorporation."

"That must have been a pretty expensive joke."

"It's no joke," Maxwellington said evenly. "They went so far as to remove the U.S.M.C. from the battalion guidons and substituted the letters Inc."

"The First Parachute Battalion, Inc."

"The Adjutant and Inspector's office couldn't revoke the charter of incorporation because it is the right of the states to grant them under the constitution, but they determined that the guidons were government property and made the men put the U.S.M.C. back on the banners and official stationery," Maxwellington explained.

"Well, so long as it doesn't interfere with their duties or the discipline of the battalion," Barrow said, "they can have their silly corporation."

"Good," Maxwellington agreed. "I don't approve of

the idea but I couldn't resist buying a few shares in it. The dividends for the first quarter of this year were twenty dollars per share."

Barrow smiled. "How many shares do you hold?"

"Two hundred," the Scotsman answered.

"Oh."

Four men walked past the two Marine officers, offering snappy salutes, which were returned. The men entered the tent where the Board of Directors were in session, opened a foot locker and took out M.P. arm brassards and white helmets of the type issued to guard companies. The clerk of the corporation (who was also the company clerk of C Company) handed the quartet official-looking passes. Grabbing submachine guns, the men left the tent and took their places on two large trucks that were parked at the end of the battalion area near the road to Nouméa.

"I'm sorry I saw that," Barrow said to Maxwellington. "That deeply disturbs me."

"The men call that special duty," Maxwellington said noncommittally. "Only the best men are given that assignment."

"Only the worst kind of man would accept it," Barrow said as he watched the trucks roll away. "Impersonating M.P.s and driving stolen trucks. Why, they're even supplied with phony credentials and orders."

"They are imaginative," Maxwellington stated. "What command won't issue them, they take. They feel that they are entitled to their Stump Juice cocktails, and they've got to get the medical alcohol."

Barrow stopped short. "My God! All the medical alcohol I've seen in the tents of the men was stolen by them. And all that other gear."

"Didn't you know?"

"I supposed it was either expended or surplus."

"As far as the paratroopers are concerned," Maxwellington said dryly, "it was both."

Barrow recalled the tender ceremonies of presentation when Corporal Martin and Pfc. Howes had delivered the case of Stump Juice to his tent, and how deeply touched he had been. The gift was nothing more than a few drops of the alcohol the paratroopers were stealing by the truckload.

"I don't think I've ever been so disappointed," he thought bitterly. "They made a fool of me."

With Maxwellington beside him, Barrow went up to the bulletin board, which stood in front of the armorer's tent, and moved aside some older notices so that he could post the communiqué from Naval Medical Headquarters. As he placed the note firmly in place, he glanced toward the tent where yesterday he had seen Marines cutting and sewing. They were still busily engaged in their work but they were not repairing parachutes.

Barrow groaned. He felt his knees slump and his shoulders sag. He was more than disappointed in what he saw. He was cruelly hurt. The material the men were using was regulation sheets, the kind found in Naval mobile hospitals and nurses quarters, and the men were cutting them into the size of flags, stenciling a large red circle in the middle and tacking down the hems. The flags were then rubbed in the dirt and treated with brown paint that resembled dried blood. An artist was adding Japanese characters.

"Genuine Japanese battle flags!" Martin's voice came to him as he stood near the bulletin board. "We'll get fifty bucks apiece for these when the fleet comes in to-morrow night."

Remembering the sentimental tears he had shed when Martin and Howes had given him the "genuine" battle flag that had flown from the top of the hill on Gavutu, Barrow now felt his eyes filling with tears of rage and embarrassment. The most treasured thing he had ever received in his life was nothing more than the bedding which probably had been stolen from a poor Navy nurse who now slept on mattress covers. The symbol of their bravery, which he had wept over, was symbolic only of their capacity as con men.

Too chagrined to enter the armorer's tent, Barrow turned to the first sergeant. "I want you to come to my office with me," he said. "I'd like some information on this organization which wasn't included in the reports you made available to me yesterday."

"Yes, sir."

In his tent, Major Barrow dropped into his chair and indicated that Maxwellington was to take the other one.

"What's wrong with this outfit?" Barrow demanded. "Why are the men such hellions and why do they have such a bum rep in Nouméa?"

"As far as Nouméa goes," Maxwellington said loyally, "I'll stack this outfit up against any other unit in the Corps and spot General Burgermeister ten Congressional Medals."

"That isn't what I meant, First Sergeant," Barrow interrupted. "Why do we have such a disciplinary problem here?"

Maxwellington paused in thought. "Well, Major," he said, "I reckon they were kept too long in action. They're all bomb-nutty. They called it shell shock in World War One."

"Is it that bad?" Barrow prodded.

"Actually, they were more than a little wacky before they went into action, judging by their service records," the Top admitted. "But in action they were superb."

"That makes up for some of their escapades," Barrow conceded.

"Yes. They took some tough terrain and neutralized some rugged Jap pushes. That earned them more medals and promotions than any other unit," Maxwellington proclaimed proudly. "They had a record for court-martials, too," he added.

"Saw quite a bit of action?"

"We landed on Gavutu on August seventh," Maxwellington said, "and with the exception of the Raiders on Tulagi, we were the only ones to see any real action in the early days of the campaign. We got pretty well shot up, and by the time we left Bloody Ridge, over on Guadalcanal, we didn't have enough men left to form a good combat team."

"So they pulled you out and sent you here to New Caledonia?" Barrow asked.

"Not exactly, sir. In those days, no one was being pulled out unless he had bones sticking through his skin," First Sergeant Maxwellington answered. "But one day a three-star general visited our area, and when he saw that all the men had placed white crosses over the heads of their foxholes, he was impressed. Later, when he saw the paratroopers out on Henderson Field trying to catch Japanese bombs in bushel baskets, he figured we had had it—and sent us here for retraining and recreation. Imagine that! Recreation on this rock. The men think he hates their guts."

"The retraining?"

"They put us to work on the waterfront of Nouméa as longshoremen. Men with open wounds," Maxwellington protested. "But that didn't last long. Too much valuable cargo turned up missing. Stuff that the paratroopers were supposed to have handled. One day the skipper of the U.S.S. *Hayes* complained that the ship's refrigerator had been stolen. Imagine that?"

"Impossible," Barrow agreed.

"Fact. Weighed tons. No one believed him. Anyway, when the merchants from this outfit began selling ice cream to the Chinese storekeepers in Nouméa, wholesale, they figured the skipper might have a case and they yanked us off the waterfront."

"And then the battalion was sent here?"

"Yes, sir. On direct orders from General Burgermeister." Maxwellington nodded. "And we haven't been bothered by anyone since. The general and his staff pulled a surprise inspection one day but he didn't stay very long. As far as we know, he never discussed the things he saw here. It must have been his junior officers who started all those crazy rumors about cannibalism and white slavery. The general was heard to compare us with the surviving mutineers of the *Bounty*, but we never had a ship in our task force by that name. I guess it was a gag."

"Tell me one thing," Barrow said. "How come the officers of this battalion haven't kept up the discipline and morale?"

"The morale is very high. The discipline is a matter of

interpretation. These men have been in action and it's hard to make them knuckle down to the old chicken routine. And the officers have been through it, too. They just pretend not to see too much. Besides, as Captain Nugent pointed out one day, if we throw all the men into the brig, who would act as guards over the prisoners?"

"As usual, Captain Nugent's logic is too advanced for me."

"I have a theory of my own," Maxwellington continued. "It's the only thing that makes life bearable for me."

"What is this theory? I might need it myself."

"The Marine Corps should never have been allowed to participate in this war. It has destroyed the Corps," Maxwellington said wisely. "But since the damage has been done, we'll have to discharge every man in this outfit as soon as the war is over and build a new Marine Corps. We'll send all these men back to civilian life and start another good old spit-and-polish organization."

"The Marine Corps shouldn't be allowed to take part in America's wars?" Barrow murmured. "Discharge the whole outfit? I'm reluctant to subscribe to that."

"It's a tough dose," Maxwellington admitted. "But if these men are allowed to stay in the Corps and set the pattern for the outfit which will be rebuilt after the war, they will corrupt untold generations of young American boys."

"That's a new twist," Barrow said thoughtfully. "I'm afraid it would take me quite a while to get conditioned to it."

"I'll give you an example of the change of values around here," Maxwellington offered. "Corporal Martin was wearing Pfc. Howes' shirt when he was reported missing in action. Martin showed up with the Third Raider Battalion in the Russells, where he helped the Raiders take the island. He was awarded two medals, but they were given to Howes because Martin was knocked out and they identified him as Howes because of the stenciling on the shirt. So Howes gets five dollars a month each for the two medals."

"I suppose that infuriates Martin."

"No. They reached a settlement. They decided the war would last another two years, so Howes gave Martin two hundred and forty dollars. Howes accepts the ten dollars medal pay each month, and if the war lasts more than two years, he stands to make a little money on the deal."

"What about the medals?" Barrow asked. "Doesn't Martin care about them? He earned them."

"The men have a philosophy about medals," Maxwellington pointed out. "They say that with one medal and ten cents, you can buy a cup of coffee."

"Values have changed, I guess," Barrow admitted. "By the way, the Russell Islands campaign is just being wrapped up. When was Martin there?"

"Last week."

"Last week! You mean he has just returned to the battalion after being over the hill since Guadalcanal?"

"Yes, sir," Maxwellington said. "But with all this business about being missing in action and his heroism while he was with the Third Raiders, Nouméa figured he'd made up for his AWOL. Actually, he made a contribution to the war effort that outweighs his Absence Without Leave."

Barrow was not listening to the end of the first sergeant's recital. He had lost interest in the capers of

Corporal Martin. But he did want to know one thing, recalling the AWOL who was commanding officer on the Tontouta strip and the AWOL who was now first sergeant at the Casual and Replacement Battalion and the AWOL who had stolen a plane to bomb Rabaul and the AWOL who had gone to New Zealand and married the politician's daughter and the AWOL who had earned two medals for his buddy while performing extra duty in the Russell Islands.

"What's the strength of this command, First Sergeant?"

"We started with four hundred and eighty men, sir," Maxwellington began.

"How many do we have now?"

"All told, about two hundred on the books."

"Where are the rest?"

"Mostly battle casualties and a few transfers."

"Of the two hundred, how many are present or can be accounted for?"

"Sometimes as many as a hundred and twenty-five."

"Oh, no! This outfit can't be that bad. No outfit can be that bad." Seventy-five AWOLs out of a battalion of two hundred! The major felt the bottom drop out of the surge of hope he had felt for the restart of his career when he had left General Burgermeister's office such a few short hours ago. He remembered the impression he expected to make on his old colleagues when he appeared among them covered with battle glory, and how, like Napoleon, he would share their woes and gladness. He had intended to get to know and understand these wonderful men. His heroes.

"They're nothing but a bunch of scoundrels," Barrow raged. "This is an organization of buccaneers, mercantile adventurers, thieves, racketeers and bootleggers."

He remembered how saddened he had been when he first viewed the thinned ranks of his battalion, thinking the outfit had been decimated by Japanese gunfire, not realizing that Absence Without Leave had accounted for most of the gaps in the lines. And Martin and his presentation of the flag that was supposed to have flown over Gavutu . . .

"To hell with this war. I quit," he bellowed. "First Sergeant, I want to be enrolled in that course in Japanese."

# 5.

Outside the tent and on the boardwalk that ran the length of the command row, Major Barrow stopped and reconsidered what he had said. A sincere and responsible officer, he was ashamed of himself—because Harold Barrow was not a quitter. True, he readily admitted to himself, he still had stars in his eyes and saw the Marine Corps in much the same boyish and romantic light which had induced him to join it, but years of service had made him aware that the outfit was more than a handsome uniform and dashing men and glamorous games. It was a fighting organization, and fighting men do not quit. His country was at war, and Marines do not lose their tempers and say to hell with war. Men who love their country and their outfit stand up and face every circumstance and fight it through. They might lose but they don't quit.

"I was angry," Barrow apologized to himself.

Good. Just what was wrong with getting angry? He should have gotten angry more often. If he had, maybe he wouldn't be carrying so much mental and physical flab. He might not have been trapped behind a desk while men with no more ability than he possessed had marched out and found what they had joined the Marine Corps to find. Glory. Honor.

Marines obey promptly and cheerfully, he had been

taught as a junior officer. But he had become so used to obeying that he had forgotten how to command. Somebody, down the line, had realized that and had sidetracked him into the position where he would not have to command. He had learned to say "Yes, sir" so well that he had denied himself the opportunity to say anything else. Until now. And he had announced that he quit.

He had believed what his instructors had said and had merged, lost, his personality and character in the demanding and impersonal profession of soldiering. Why, he had become a yes man—and, of course, yes men become clerks.

When was the last time he had allowed himself to become angry? It was before he had joined the Marine Corps. Once he had not devoted himself to the pleasing and yessing of authority. He did things the way *he* thought they should be done. When steel blades flashed against the ice and sticks of ash lashed out against man and puck, he had fought to win. He had spent many long and miserable minutes in the penalty box for asserting himself, but when the score was tallied, he had led his team to victory. He had let himself get angry and, in anger, he had fought to win.

Fine. He would let himself become angry now, and he would remain angry. He felt good about it. He had made a decision, the first important one in a long time, and he felt his mind quicken to the point of thrill. He had regained something he had lost, something valuable. His shoulders responded by straightening and his chest advanced forward. Barrow wouldn't quit. Like John Paul Jones, he had not yet begun to fight.

"Maxwellington was right," he told himself. "This

outfit is overripe for a stiff treatment of the old Corps discipline. And that it shall get."

He tried to think of something sensible to do to start his disciplinary ball rolling. Aggravating himself by deliberately recalling the brazenness and audacity of the men who manufactured their own Japanese battle flags and operated stills of industrial proportions and demolitioned Quonset huts for whiskey between trips to the docks to empty cargo ships of medical alcohol, he could not form a single thought or practical idea. Swell. Commanding officers do not have to be practical. He filled his lungs and shouted across the area:

"Now hear this. Every officer in this battalion is confined to quarters and every enlisted man is designated a prisoner-at-large."

"That will hold them until I get my thoughts organized," Barrow assured himself as he retired to his tent.

Hearing the major's shout, Captain Nugent rushed from the Officer of the Day's tent to join First Sergeant Maxwellington. "What happened?" he asked in alarm.

"The usual," Maxwellington said sadly. "He got the word on the battalion. Like all the rest who came up here, he'll be gone in the morning."

"Gee, he didn't even last two days."

"Yes." Maxwellington nodded. "It's too bad. He was a nice fellow."

"That's right," Nugent agreed. "I kind of liked him."

In their tents, the enlisted men of the battalion listened to Barrow's explosion, looked at each other, shrugged their shoulders and continued making Japanese battle flags and writing new verses to the "Marine's Hymn."

"There goes another one," Martin said to Howes.

"Yeah," Howes responded. "It's a pity. The quality of

officers they send out here is pathetic. The Marine Corps has no more leadership above the rank of sergeant."

"Who needs officers, anyway?" Private Lincoln intoned. "They only clutter up."

"That old slob seemed like a nice guy, though," Sergeant Fogleman said. "I thought he'd stay at least a week."

"Maybe the next one will."

"Maybe . . . " Corporal Crocker spoke for the men. "It sure would be nice if we could have a permanent commanding officer again."

"It sure would," the men agreed without hope.

> "If the Army or the Navy
> Ever look on Heaven's scenes,
> They will find their wives are sleeping
> With the United States Marines,"

the Board of Directors of the First Parachute Battalion, Inc., sang as Major Barrow fell asleep.

Major Barrow did not leave his tent until the next morning. It was a grim and determined commanding officer who entered the tent of the Officer of the Day and shouted, "Captain Nugent! Get up and have one of the field musics blow reveille."

"The field musics are over the hill," Nugent answered, surprised to see Barrow still in the area. "They ran away with a U.S.O. unit."

"Then you get up and break out the noncoms," Barrow said imperatively. "I want to address the men immediately after the roll is taken."

"Yes, sir."

The major watched as the men stumbled out of their

tents and formed ragged lines down the length of the street across from the command section. After the order, "Dress right—Dress," the platoon sergeants called off the names of the troopers and relayed their tallies to the platoon leaders, who formally reported to the company commanders. The company commanders advised the major that one hundred and eighteen men were present or could be accounted for.

Major Barrow stepped in front of the men of the battalion, pudgy fists on his bulging hips, and stared sternly at the paratroopers.

"I respect and admire you men because of your wonderful battle records," he began. "I am proud to be a member of so distinguished an organization."

"You know," Crocker told Fogleman, "that guy is utterly correct."

"Yes," Fogleman agreed. "He is very discerning."

"But I deplore your conduct between battles," Barrow continued. "You seem determined to neutralize your combat accomplishments by reducing this Marine base to a home for wayward boys. Your actions are becoming a disgrace, and the things you did up north do not excuse the propensity for delinquency you have demonstrated in New Caledonia."

"What he say?" Corporal Martin asked.

"I'm not sure," Pfc. Howes answered. "I think we're getting another Presidential Unit Citation."

"So there's going to be some changes made around here," Barrow threatened. "This organization is going to become a part of the Marine Corps again and you are going to learn to conduct yourselves as Marines. I am going to ask you to take this war seriously and retrain accordingly."

"The sun got him," Private Lincoln observed.

"Or the moon."

"The First Parachute Battalion is going to be run by the Book," Barrow went on. "It's going to be run like every other unit in the Corps. And I'm going to run it."

"He must have seen some of those Marine movies," Martin muttered. "He's got himself mixed up with Wallace Beery."

"I'll bet he's a sailor in disguise," Crocker added.

"Beginning with office hours," Barrow said, "every one of you men will be assigned duties. These duties will be of a military nature. There shall be no more cocktail hours or meetings of the Board of Directors. You will cease and desist from unloading cargo ships and the manufacture of phony Japanese equipment for sale to tourists and sailors. The alcohol, cigars, cigarettes, candy and all other stolen gear in this battalion is to be turned over to the division quartermaster, and you are going to give the nurses back their sheets."

"I knew it," the morale officer's assistant moaned. "He's a saboteur."

"He must be a German," Howes agreed. "The Japs aren't that bad."

"Immediately after chow," Barrow concluded, dismissing the men, "all of you will remain in your tents for inspection."

"Why do we always get the crackpots?" a company clerk asked in simple wonder.

"We could rig up a land mine for him to step on," Private Lincoln planned. "That would save him and us a lot of trouble."

The major's inspection of the area was the terror of the battalion for weeks. Accompanied by Captain Nugent, whom Barrow reluctantly appointed as his adjutant, and First Sergeant Maxwellington, the commanding officer left a wake of havoc on his brief but relentless cruise of the enlisted men's area.

Pfc. Howes reported to Corporal Crocker. "The official count is two hundred and ten," he groaned.

"The beast," Crocker snarled.

But it was true. Major Barrow had ripped up two hundred and ten indecent Parisian pin-up pictures and thrown the naked likenesses into the streets.

Sadly the men drifted into the battalion streets and surveyed the carnage that identified the route of the new commanding officer. The signs that had hung over the front of the tents were splintered and strewn in the dirt.

"Please, sir"—Captain Nugent had intervened for the men at one point—"let the men keep their pin-ups of Kathy Kennedy. Why, she's a combination of Lana Turner, Betty Grable and Dorothy Lamour. She has dimensions that even her press agent doesn't dare to release. She's the only reason they're in this war."

"I don't suppose they ever heard of Hitler or Tojo," Barrow snarled. "But they can keep their pin-ups as long as the pictures are decent."

"Now how could there be anything indecent about a girl as lovely as that?" Nugent pondered, admiring a busty picture of the beautiful actress.

"You, too, have the soul of an artist," Barrow said in disgust.

Eighteen jeeps were taken away from careless paratroopers who drove the vehicles into the battalion area, and enough alcohol and grapefruit juice were delivered to the Naval hospitals to supply the sickbays for months.

Within a week, twenty men had been arraigned for courts-martial, five sergeants were busted to corporals and eleven corporals were reduced to privates.

But the worst thing he did, as far as the paratroopers were concerned, was to put them to work. He assigned working parties and guard duty to every man in the battalion. In the hot tropical sun, on his direct orders, which they could not disobey, men stood rigidly at attention in front of the brig or near the Quonset hut and looked longingly at the river they could not enter. Platoons of men kicked up New Caledonia dust as they performed the maneuvers of troop and drill in the company streets, and groups of paratroopers fulfilled the police details formerly left to gangs of hired Kanakas. Classes were held every midmorning and midafternoon on such subjects as demolition and explosives, compass reading, small arms and military courtesy.

"Did you hear?" Pfc. Howes lamented as he ran a swab through the bore of his rifle. "He has inaugurated a sunset march in review."

"I ain't stood one of those since Smedley Butler was commanding general of the Quantico barracks," Fogleman recalled. "Back in the thirties."

"You ain't heard nothing," Crocker griped. "He's taken away our week-end passes and we're going on another overnight forced march."

"Somebody ought to tell him there's a war on."

But the period of intensive retraining was doing the First Parachute Battalion a world of good. And the Marine who got the most out of it was Major Harold Barrow. Grunting and panting up the hills of New Caledonia, Barrow left many pounds of his excess weight on the trails. He was happily forced to punch holes in his belt to keep his trousers up as his waistline abated, and one day he joyously rediscovered his hip bones. His waddle gradually changed until there was a semblance of swagger in his walk, and the once prominent cheekbones, now bronzed by the tropical sun, again dominated his face. His carbine hung comfortably from the shoulders that were losing their roundness. He looked less like a milk bottle.

The men obeyed Barrow's commands as Marines must, but they showed less and less enthusiasm for him and his reform program. They thought he was foolish and regretted that he, of all the commanding officers sent to Tontouta, had to be the one to stick it out. After his first day with the battalion, they never again asked him to join their cocktail hour.

# 6.

These were not happy days for Major Barrow. He was doing his duty as he saw it, and was sure that his efforts were directed toward the best interests of the men of his battalion and his country. And if the period of intensive training was tough for the troops, it was more so for him. They, at least, had each other to lean on, to share complaints. He was alone, disliked by the men he still, deep down, respected and admired. A good leader needs, and should enjoy, the affection of his men. He might gain that in time. Maybe. In the meantime, the cold hard fact of war prevailed and he applied himself to that arduous circumstance. That took all his energy, thoughts and time.

It was almost more than he could bear, therefore, when First Sergeant Maxwellington delivered more unpleasant news—news which could mean another ugly situation.

"General Burgermeister just called up, Major Barrow," the Top announced. "He's always furious, but this time it sounds like he's been eating Navy soup."

"Why should he be furious at me?" Barrow asked.

"I don't know, sir, but you better get to Nouméa."

As the major entered Burgermeister's office, he was surprised to see another general there. General Belanger, head of the Free French forces on the island, was staring glumly out the window, and it was apparent that relations between him and the Marine general were less than cordial. A short man, almost tiny, and with a thin mustache that quivered in anger, he whirled toward Major Barrow as the paratroopers' commander came to attention in front of the desk.

"Here is the man who has made this a three-sided war," Belanger snarled at Burgermeister. "America's answer to Napoleon."

"Ah, yes," Burgermeister agreed, swinging red and vicious eyes on the major. "Our second Pearl Harbor."

"What's the matter, General?" Barrow implored. "What happened?"

"Apparently your political ambitions exceed anything the Marine Corps can offer you, Major!" Burgermeister sneered. "You must find manipulating one little battalion very boring."

"Oh, no, sir," Barrow assured the general. "I'm very content with my command. It's practically a new outfit since I took it over."

"I believe that," Burgermeister boomed. "Before you went to Tontouta, I wasn't exactly sure whose side the paratroopers were on in this war. Now I know. Under your careful tutelage, they have gone all the way over to the Japs."

"That's not true, sir."

"You have succeeded in doing something the entire Nazi army could not accomplish," Belanger screamed at Barrow. "The motherland, yes. The Germans conquered that temporarily. But it took you and your hoodlums to dismantle the French empire."

"I don't understand, sir."

"Didn't you know"—Burgermeister lowered his voice to an ominous whisper—"that the men of your outfit have induced the natives of New Caledonia to politically align themselves with the United States?"

"I don't know what you mean, sir."

"Your menagerie has prevailed upon the Kanakas and Javanese on this island to petition the government officials of New Caledonia to consent to a referendum in which they can express their desire to be admitted into our Union as the forty-ninth state. The State of New Caledonia, U.S.A."

"The forty-ninth state? New Caledonia?"

"Yes. They're not even willing to defer to Alaska or Hawaii."

"France's empire is being stripped by her allies," Belanger shrieked.

"This is the first time it has been brought to my attention, sir," Barrow explained. "I'll have my men stop this nonsense immediately."

"It's too late," Belanger said, on the verge of hysterics. "Your Sergeant Fogleman has promised every New Caledonian voter a jeep. We French can never erase that dream from the Kanaka's mind. He'd sell his place in heaven for a jeep. So the loyalty of the natives is forever lost to France."

"Has Sergeant Fogleman really stolen that many jeeps?" Burgermeister demanded of Major Barrow.

"I doubt it, sir."

"He might be in the position to keep his promise," the Marine general pointed out, "if the rest of his scheme is successful."

"What would that be, General?"

"He has announced his candidacy to stand for election

to the United States Senate to represent this island in Washington," Burgermeister answered, his voice growing loud again. "And do you know who has been selected as his running mate for the other seat?"

"No, sir."

"You, you renegade!"

"Permit me," the French general said pompously, unrolling a large sheet of paper. He spread it out on Burgermeister's desk, and Barrow recoiled in horror. Printed in bold red and blue type against a white background was the appeal: "Burst the bonds of European tyranny. Send Major Barrow and Sergeant Fogleman to the United States Senate." Alongside the grinning portrait of Sergeant Fogleman was a picture of the major squinting owlishly at the voters.

"I don't believe it," Barrow groaned. "It's impossible."

"Nothing is impossible with the paratroopers," General Burgermeister contradicted.

"But, sir . . ."

Burgermeister pushed the political poster aside and clamped his eyes on the major's. "The last push left the First Marine Division considerably undermanned," he said evenly, "and I have been instructed by Washington to reshuffle some of my units to consolidate the division's strength. I am so fed up with the antics of your men that I have seriously considered merging them into the First Raider Battalion."

"Please, sir, don't do that."

"Out of respect to Colonel Edson and his splendid battalion," the general continued, "I have abandoned that idea. But I might transfer your whole zoo to some other outfit."

"I guarantee the good behavior of my men," Barrow pleaded. "It would kill them to lose their battalion."

"And it would kill me to lose the war in this theater," Burgermeister went on. "Your outfit gives me more trouble than all the rest of the division, and this affair of the forty-ninth state is the limit. If one more complaint is lodged against your animal farm, you go back to Washington and the paratroopers will be disbanded."

"Yes, sir."

"And as if I didn't have enough trouble trying to run a theater of war against a formidable enemy and keeping up with the escapades of your three-ring circus," Burgermeister concluded, "the complete disruption of friendly relations between my office and our allies has filled my life to the brim. I can't take any more. Now, get out of my sight."

"If those paratroopers cross my path once more," Barrow heard Belanger threaten Burgermeister as he hurried down the hall, "I am going to negotiate a separate peace with the Japanese."

"That won't be necessary," Burgermeister told the Frenchman. "This will blow over."

"I'm not so sure. Under my wartime powers I can refuse to allow a referendum, but my political enemies will make great capital out of this affair," Belanger said, outlining his position.

"You don't have any enemies comparable to the Japs."

"Oh, yes, I do," Belanger contradicted. "You know the Vichy problem was never completely solved here. The remainder of the Vichy gang and my old peacetime foes seize on anything to discredit me."

"They're still not as formidable as the Japanese."

"Not to you," Belanger corrected, "but with me it's a running fight. The Vichy element and my prewar opponents are always out to get me. They'll stop at nothing."

"The Marines stand behind you, General," Burgermeister assured his colleague.

"I know. That's what worries me."

After Belanger left his office, General Burgermeister eased himself into his canvas chair. "I wonder if the Japanese High Command has any problems similar to mine," he muttered. "I guess not, because I never heard of any Japanese paratroopers."

His thoughts were interrupted by Colonel Ward knocking at the door.

"Well?" Burgermeister sighed.

"It's about Private Sigmund Yankowitz, sir. He's here."

"That's all I need," Burgermeister fumed. "Show him in."

After a brief interview with Private Yankowitz, Burgermeister called for his orderly. "Make out this man's papers for a transfer to the First Parachute Battalion"—he grinned—"and call my jeep. I'll take him to Tontouta myself."

In the battalion streets, Major Barrow shouted for his men to assemble.

"Fogleman," he began sternly, "what could you have been thinking of?"

"It was all Corporal Crocker's fault, sir," Fogleman alibied. "He put the vodka into the Coca-Cola at the lawn party, and the French ladies . . ."

"That's not what I'm talking about."

"Has he been renting rooms in the French army barracks to Navy nurses again?" Captain Nugent asked.

"No," First Sergeant Maxwellington answered. "I know what he did. He got General Belanger's daughter looped last night and had her do a can-can in the lobby of the Hotel Metropole. The general and his staff came just as she was doing her high kicks. He put the hotel off limits this morning."

"Quiet," Barrow demanded. He turned angrily to Fogleman. "You have no business meddling in the politics of New Caledonia."

"What did he do?" Captain Nugent prodded, concerned because Fogleman belonged to his company.

"He's trying to get New Caledonia to join our Union," Barrow complained, "and he has entered himself and me as candidates for the United States Senate. Belanger and Burgermeister are in a white heat."

Nugent looked at his sergeant and shook his head. "You're a troublemaker, Fogleman," he said severely, "but if you make the Senate, you'll need a legislative assistant and I've always wanted to . . ."

"Please, Captain Nugent," Barrow interrupted, anxious to resume control of his lecture.

Private Lincoln stepped out of the ranks and approached the major, offering him his hand. "Good luck," the gloomy private offered. "Don't forget your old friends."

Barrow ignored Lincoln and demanded of Fogleman, "Why did you put my name on that poster? Why did you propose me for the United States Senate?"

"A concession to the brass." Fogleman shrugged.

"Good politics." Crocker nodded in agreement.

"Who's going to represent the island in the House of

Representatives?" Corporal Martin inquired. "I'm available."

"Attention!" Barrow shouted. "Listen to me."

The men listened, shocked by Barrow's shout.

"Fogleman," the major proceeded, "you're restricted to the area."

"Did I do something wrong?" Fogleman defended himself. "What are we fighting for?"

"Not to field strip the French empire while the French are fighting by our side," Barrow said heatedly.

"German or French," Fogleman persisted, "what's the difference? Empires are old-fashioned and undemocratic. While we're over here, we might as well do the job right."

"He's right." Captain Nugent nodded gravely.

"No, he's not," Barrow pointed out. "We are fighting the Japs and the Germans at this time. Not the French."

"Why are we fighting the Germans and the Japanese?" Nugent countered.

"Because they have taken the land of other nations and oppressed the people."

"Right!" Fogleman agreed in triumph. "And that's exactly what has happened in New Caledonia. Frenchmen, go home!"

Barrow groaned. "That is an issue which is not for you to decide," he lashed out at Fogleman. "Leave the French alone."

"It's disgraceful," Private Lincoln put in. "We're always making concessions to the French."

"Maybe we can liberate Australia from the British," Howes offered as compensation to his crestfallen friend Fogleman.

"That would be fine," Barrow said sarcastically. "But wait until we have liberated the Philippines."

"Okay." Fogleman went along with the gag. "If you really feel strongly about it."

"Thank you, Sergeant."

"You're welcome, Major."

"If you think you can take it," First Sergeant Maxwellington told Major Barrow as they walked toward the office, "I have another bit of bad news for you."

"After what I just went through," Barrow corrected, "anything would be good news."

"Yes, sir," Maxwellington said, "but I just found out something."

"Proceed."

"The men didn't turn in all their prisoners before they left the Solomons."

"I haven't the slightest idea what you're talking about."

"The men in C Company held out three prisoners and smuggled them back here. They're using the Nips for houseboys. They've taught them to mix Stump Juice cocktails and they've dressed them in white coats." Maxwellington waited for Barrow's reaction.

"Is that all?"

"Yes, sir."

"Have the Japs turned loose. Get them out of here."

"Do you realize what you're saying," Maxwellington gasped. "Those are enemy troops."

"Yes, I fully realize what I'm saying," Barrow said determinedly. "I've only been out here a short time and I've already been threatened with a trip back to the States as a misfit. After the ultimatum I just received from the general, I'd be on the next boat if he ever suspected this battalion is harboring the enemy."

"But, sir . . ."

"If you think I'm going to take them to headquarters and explain to General Burgermeister where I got them, you're crazy. Slip them into the woods."

"I won't have time now," Maxwellington said, pointing toward the highway. "Here comes General Burgermeister now."

General Burgermeister, driving with his red and gold flag flapping in the breeze, pulled into the area. Beside him was a Marine private.

"Look what I've brought you," Burgermeister boomed, nodding toward his passenger. "This is Private Sigmund Yankowitz."

Barrow glanced at Private Yankowitz. The young man was well over six feet six inches, the tallest Marine Barrow had ever seen.

"Show the major your papers, Yankowitz." The general smiled sweetly.

Major Barrow studied the private's transfer order, confusion spreading over his face. "Why, General," he said, "these orders say that Private Yankowitz is to report to the Post Service Battalion in Quantico, Virginia."

"That's right," the general confirmed gleefully.

"Well, what's he doing here?"

"That's a good question. No one told him to get off the train from Parris Island, South Carolina, when it stopped at Quantico," the general explained, "so he rode all the way to San Francisco. He didn't know what to do there, so he stood on the docks for six weeks. And then one day he saw a body of Marines getting on a transport and he fell in with them and sailed to New Zealand. He didn't know anyone in New Zealand and couldn't find any place that even sounded like Quantico, so he joined another outfit that was going aboard the *Matsonia*. Fortunately, for us, that ship landed here and Yankowitz was picked up on the waterfront in Nouméa. I knew you'd love to have a man of such resourcefulness in your command."

"Ahem." Barrow stalled for time while he organized his thoughts. "Couldn't we find him transportation to Quantico, somehow."

"A good idea, Barrow," the general said, "but why bother? The Post Service Battalions generally get the sick, the lame and the lazy. It takes about fifteen years in the Marines to qualify for a service battalion—by getting kicked out of every other outfit from Panama to Iceland. The personnel officer at Parris Island must have been a prophet to send this man to such a lash-up direct from boot camp. Save all the others fifteen years of hell, judging by my first impression of Yankowitz. But now that he's here, I thought you and your men might give him your postgraduate course at the outset of his career so that when he gets to a service battalion he'll feel right at home."

"Yes, sir."

"Private Yankowitz," Burgermeister said, "this is Major Barrow."

Yankowitz came around the jeep and walked smartly up to Major Barrow, but instead of saluting, he grabbed his new commanding officer by the hand and began shaking it. "Hi, Corporal," he said, "glad to meet you. I think we'll get along okay. I can tell you're a wheel around here and I like to get to know the wheels. Just call me Ziggy."

The mountains of New Caledonia rang with the roar of Burgermeister's laughter. "Ain't he a beaut, Barrow? I knew you'd love him."

"Do you suppose fifteen days on bread and water would smarten this man up, Corporal—I mean, Major?" the first sergeant asked.

"Don't bother," Barrow said.

While the general looked on and smiled, Major Barrow tried to get better acquainted with his new man. He learned that Yankowitz had spent all his productive years in a coal mine in Joppa, Pennsylvania, and had never left that small town before enlisting in the Marine Corps. The only thing that the private expressed any interest in was his beloved mines, and when Barrow, not knowing much about them, couldn't hold up his end of the conversation, Yankowitz became uninterested in the major and drifted off to acquaint himself with his new bunkies.

"Nice-looking area you have here," Burgermeister observed. "Why don't you show me around, Barrow?"

"I'm sure the general is too busy," Barrow stammered, wanting only to be rid of his nemesis.

"I've got all day," Burgermeister assured him.

With the major behind him, General Burgermeister strode across the company streets and peered into one of the tents, where a group of paratroopers were sitting on bunks, sipping drinks from canteen cups. The general stepped inside the tent and Barrow followed him.

"Hi," one of the troopers said. "Have a drink?"

"Love to," Burgermeister answered, trying not to

show the anger he felt when no one showed enough respect for his rank even to stand.

He and Major Barrow were handed brimming canteen cups by a little man in a white coat.

"Thank you," Burgermeister said. He turned to Barrow. "Nothing like a big cool drink of juice on a hot day." He took a long swallow and then left the bunk he was sitting on and came to full attention.

"Wow!" he shouted. "What was that?"

"Alcohol and grapefruit juice," Barrow answered, wondering how much of the stuff had escaped him on his inspection. "The men call it Stump Juice."

The general had a reputation for being tough and he wanted to live up to it, so he resumed his seat and sipped on his cocktail.

He looked up when two more small men in white coats entered the tent and began to pour cans of grapefruit juice into a tin of medical alcohol. He looked again at the men and once more came to full attention.

"Japs!" he bellowed.

The thunder of his voice caused several of the men to drop their canteen cups and others to jump for their rifles. The men in the white coats dived under the nearest cots, petrified with fear by the booming voice of the general. They had little English and thought it was a bombing raid.

"I don't believe it," Burgermeister shouted as he dragged the Japanese out from under the bunks. "It can't be."

"Our houseboys," Corporal Martin volunteered.

"Yes," Fogleman confirmed. "We hired them in the Solomons."

"Houseboys! Friendly troops from the Solomons!"

General Burgermeister had never had an experience such as this. "These are refugees from the Japanese Imperial Army. This is fantastic."

The houseboys, hissing through their teeth, bowed low before the general. "Tojo is a meathead," they said, one of the phrases of English the Marines had taught them. And, trying to be helpful, they added, "General Burgermeister is a meathead."

Burgermeister dashed to the entrance of the tent. "Guards!" he roared. "Where are the guards?"

Two men on guard duty rushed up, rifles on the ready, bayonets fixed. "What's the matter, sir?" they asked.

"Japs!" Burgermeister shouted.

The guards looked around for a place to hide. "Where, General?"

"In that tent. Bring them out and lock them up."

"Oh, them Japs," the guards said in relief. "Those are our houseboys."

"I want them in Nouméa in thirty minutes or you'll be houseboys in Portsmouth Prison for the next thirty years."

"But, sir," the guards protested. "They're domesticated."

"Don't argue with me," Burgermeister shrieked. "Arrest them."

"Yes, sir."

"And, Major Barrow," Burgermeister boomed, "assemble these characters on the double. I want a word with these slave marketeers."

The men shifted from one foot to the other under the withering glances of the infuriated general. Barrow stood in a stuttering coma.

"Barrow," Burgermeister raged, "I should have you shot."

"I'm sorry about it, sir," Barrow said numbly. "It was a mistake."

"Yes," Burgermeister agreed vehemently. "This whole war seems to be a mistake."

"Yes, sir," Barrow replied stupidly. "A failure in diplomacy."

Burgermeister gritted his teeth and turned to the paratroopers. "I have a good mind to shame you people by sending you back to the States in disgrace . . ."

A thunderous cheer of approval filled the air.

"Yes, sir," Captain Nugent said, nodding toward the men, "that would be a fine way to punish us."

"We can be ready in fifteen minutes," Corporal Crocker advised from the ranks.

"Besides," Private Lincoln added, "we're yellow."

Burgermeister pressed his hands against his temples and continued. ". . . or transfer the whole bunch of you to the Fifth Marines."

"Not the Fifth, sir," Sergeant Fogleman pleaded. "They're stupid."

"They're not stupid," Burgermeister lashed back. "They are fine men."

"They're Marines, aren't they?" Fogleman pressed.

"Yes," the Marine general agreed, "they're Marines."

"Well," Fogleman said smugly. "If they weren't stupid, they wouldn't be Marines."

"He's got a point there," Captain Nugent observed.

His head spinning from the effects of the alcohol and tropical sun and the weird logic of the paratroopers, Burgermeister staggered toward his jeep. "Let me get out of here," he mumbled to himself, clashing the gears, "before I go to pieces. This must be a terrible dream."

Major Barrow felt no better than the general. Still stunned by the ultimatum he had received in General Belanger's presence, and the awful visit of General Burgermeister, he walked blindly through his camp, shaking his head, trying to get matters back into perspective.

"What have I gotten myself into?" he groaned. "Is it possible that all this misery is happening to me? What did I do to deserve it?"

# 7.

Major Barrow's spirits picked up considerably as he wandered through the tent rows a few days later. The wonderfully clean streets and the neatness of the men's pyramidals again indicated to him that his troopers were Marines, and, under proper leadership, could be reclaimed—disciplined—into a compliant military organization. He had made some headway in this awesome task but was increasingly aware that the actual depth of his paratroopers' connivings was still not known to him. Japanese houseboys!

Glancing into the pyramidals, he noted the perfectly made bunks and the orderliness of the men's gear. The top blankets on the cots were taut as drumheads, the shoes properly placed together and the rifles neatly racked. But halfway down one company street he paused, noticing that the bunks were unmade in the rest of the tents to the end of the line. In one pyramidal he saw a pair of slim legs busily walking around a bunk. The legs belonged to a girl. She was tucking in blankets and, when finished, moved on to the next unmade bed. She winked at him.

"Who are you?" Barrow demanded, "and what are you doing in this area?"

"I'm Marie," the black-haired, bright-eyed girl answered with a smile. "I'm the new maid."

"Maid?" Barrow looked down on the girl, blushing as he found himself staring at the bold, up-thrust lines of her lovely figure. "How long have the men had a maid?"

"I don't know." Her dazzling smile almost blinded the major. "A girl friend of mine once worked for them for four months. She had to leave because she is indisposed. She is going to have a . . ."

"Ahem," Major Barrow interrupted. "You'll have to leave this camp immediately. We can't have a girl among all these men."

"Now where could there be a better place for a girl to be than among men." Marie giggled, bending over to tuck in the blanket on a bunk, accenting the lovely roundness of her hips as Barrow tried to look away. "And such handsome men!"

"Regardless," Barrow said, loosing his collar, "I want you to leave this place. I don't want any women around here."

"How long have you been in the Marine Corps?" The girl again showed the major the whiteness of her teeth in a gay smile. "You don't talk like any Marine I ever met."

"I'll arrange for your transportation right away," Barrow said determinedly. "You must leave this camp."

"Well, I shall not leave this camp," the girl said firmly. "I have a contract."

Barrow escorted the maid back to the command section. Captain Nugent looked up from his desk in the adjutant's office as Barrow entered with the lady.

"Hello, Marie," Nugent greeted her.

"Did you know this girl was in our camp, Nugent?" Barrow asked, shocked.

"Yes, sir. I should. I paid my two dollars."

Barrow's face turned as red as a Marine guidon. "What kind of a man are you? What kind of a girl is this?"

Captain Nugent explained. "We all chip in two dollars each month to pay for maid service."

"Houseboys. Rifle bearers. Kanaka street sweepers and now maid service." Barrow murmured. "Is this a hotel?"

"And Marie is a fine girl," Captain Nugent continued. "Her father is General Belanger."

Barrow collapsed into the canvas chair. "General Belanger's daughter! If he finds out his daughter is here, he'll hang me. He'll have us all guillotined."

"Oh, I don't know," Captain Nugent soothed the major.

"Well, I do," Barrow stated. "He hates paratroopers."

"He won't know where I am unless you tell him." Marie smiled sweetly at the major, moving near him, smothering him in her perfume and beauty. "I bribed a signalman on the *Missouri* to flash a message off the stern of the ship as it pulled out for the north. Father thinks I'm aboard the battleship, a guest of Admiral Dorsey. And the *Big Mo* is going into action near the Slot and can't send or receive messages. It won't be back for at least a month."

"That doesn't make any difference," Barrow said in desperation. "You've got to get out of here."

"I've got a contract," Marie insisted.

"What's this business about a contract?" Barrow asked the Captain.

"Well, we expect certain services of Marie, such as

bedmaking and sweeping, and because we pay her a month's salary in advance, we demanded a contract. The contract works both ways."

"Well, I'm sorry . . ." Barrow began.

"I'll sue . . ." Marie anticipated his remark. Her black eyes sparkled as she raised her face to the major's. "I'll tell my father that you're trying to cheat me out of my wages."

"Young lady," Barrow said sternly, "this is a Marine camp, not a dude ranch. Marine camps are governed by rules and regulations which do not permit . . ."

"You're cute," she cut him short.

Barrow leaned back in the chair and shook his head. Why, he asked himself, was he always getting mixed up in the weirdest kind of situation and with the oddest people. However, he quickly amended his thoughts, the only odd thing about this girl was her remarkable beauty and her presence in an all-male community. He had been immediately aware of the unusual loveliness of the young lady and, if it weren't for the circumstances, he would have been much more tolerant of her being in his camp. If only she weren't a general's daughter and if only regulations did not prohibit women in a military installation . . .

He certainly did not want any more trouble with General Belanger. Marie had threatened to tell her father that he was cheating her out of her pay, and regardless of what she told the general, she would surely disclose that she had lived in his camp among his men. Belanger would have a fit. And Barrow couldn't just toss her out of the base. Why couldn't he? Well, he didn't want to.

While seeking a resolution, he studied the girl. That

was a pleasant occupation. He guessed she was in her twenties. She was as pretty as only a healthy and happy French girl can be. Her bright black eyes were positively radiant and her dark hair accentuated her smooth and glowing complexion. And she had a wonderful, almost athletic, shape. Her shoulders seemed wider because of the narrowness of her hips and waist. Her full breasts and long straight legs completed the lovely apparition she presented to the major. Naturally, he formed absolutely no thoughts pertaining to his predicament as he looked at her.

Marie had a few ideas regarding the Marine major sitting across from her. He was nice. He wasn't as suave and gracious as the Frenchmen in Nouméa, but that was refreshing. He surely was not as bold as the enlisted Marines, and that was too bad. But she liked his looks, the strength he reflected after weeks of tough physical training, and the open honesty she saw in his eyes. He was a good man. Just a little pompous and too serious, maybe, but a decent sort, this officer. She liked him, and instead of making any contribution to solving the problem they faced, wondered, instead, how she might break through his reserve. She supposed she'd have to meet this man more than halfway, and she was ready and willing to do that. It would be fun and he really was cute.

Reluctantly, Major Barrow snapped his mind back to the business of finding a decision. He wasn't overly disappointed when his thoughts were interrupted.

"Major Barrow," the voice of First Sergeant Maxwellington called, "the M.P.s have Corporal Crocker under arrest. They want to make a report to you."

Barrow excused himself and went to meet the two husky M.P.s who had Corporal Crocker between them.

The Marine cops were looking respectfully at their prisoner, apparently reluctant to make their report.

"What's the matter?" Barrow asked the M.P.s.

Without preliminaries, one M.P. said, "With General Burgermeister's knowledge and consent, the Allied Forces have put the entire island of New Caledonia off limits to your paratroopers. They are confined to this area."

"My compliments to the general," Barrow answered, "and why is this whole country off limits to my men?"

"The Admiral of the Fleet initiated a complaint, sir," the M.P. explained, "and General Belanger of the Free French lodged a similar one. They concern the conducted tour Corporal Crocker of your command arranges for Navy personnel."

"Conducted tour of what?"

"The island of New Caledonia."

Barrow turned to the corporal. "What's this nonsense about a conducted tour, Corporal Crocker?"

"Well, sir," Crocker answered, "the sailors don't care too much for the U.S.O., and the Red Cross doesn't offer much in the way of entertainment . . ."

"So you're filling the gap?"

"He sure is," the M.P. said. "Boy, I wish I could take his tour."

"Suppose you fill me in on this fabulous tour," Major Barrow suggested. "If it's as good as you say, I might take it myself."

"Well, to begin with," the M.P. said, "you can't take the tour. Only sailors."

"Why?"

"According to Crocker, only sailors are rich enough and stupid enough to take it."

"Tell me about the tour."

"Corporal Crocker hires a bus from a Frenchman in Nouméa and parks it by the Navy landing," the M.P. explained. "He jams fifty sailors into the bus and charges them twenty-five dollars each."

"He makes twelve hundred and fifty dollars? Wow!"

"That ain't half of it, sir. He guarantees to stop at ten bars—all bootleg joints—and one house of ill repute," the M.P. went on. "And he does."

"Oh, no."

"Oh, yes," the M.P. contradicted. "And he has a working arrangement with the bars where he stops. He manufactures the anisette that is served to the sailors. He sells it to the bar owners and he also gets a cut of the business he brings in. They say that he owns three of the joints outright. He also gets a percentage of the proceeds realized by the Pink House."

"Pink House?"

"That's the house of ill repute."

"I think I've heard enough," Barrow said, dismissing the M.P.s, who turned to go. Then, "Wait a minute," he called. "I forgot to ask you why General Belanger registered a complaint."

"Corporal Crocker carries several sets of binoculars to allow his customers a close-up of the highlights of the tour," the M.P. answered. "General Belanger blew his stack when he discovered that fifty sailors were looking in his bedroom window while his wife prepared for bed. He sure didn't admire the comments the sailors made about her. She's kind of plump."

"I don't think she's as fat as the sailors say," Corporal Crocker offered helpfully.

A horrible thought occurred to Major Barrow. "You

said the admiral initiated a complaint? I thought he was on the *Missouri* and headed for the Slot."

"It was a feint. He'll be in port for a week."

Barrow winced.

"A lot of action when he pulled in last night," the M.P. said. "As soon as she dropped the hook, General Belanger was aboard, and he raised hell. Seems the *Big Mo* pulled out with something on it that belonged to him. All the ship's signalmen are in chains."

"Good-bye."

Barrow hurried to rejoin Captain Nugent and the pretty maid in the tent. Knowing he must keep his head in what seemed to be a dire emergency, he controlled his temper.

"The U.S.S. *Missouri* is in port," he announced dramatically, "and General Belanger has already been aboard her. The ship's signalmen have been put under arrest."

The captain and the general's daughter shared Barrow's concern.

"What should we do?" Captain Nugent asked. "We can't merely turn Marie loose in Nouméa. Her father would lower the boom on her for lying and running away."

"That," Barrow said emphatically, "is no concern of mine. I don't want the general lowering the boom on me, either."

"Whatever we do," Nugent said, "we can't get started until after dark."

"And if the signalmen on the *Missouri* sing," Marie pointed out, "Father will be up here before then."

"I hate to even think in such terms," Barrow said, "but I have no alternative. I believe we should have the men take Marie aboard the *Missouri* after dark and leave her there. That's where she's supposed to be, and I don't even want to be suspected of harboring her."

"The paratroopers will be able to get her on the ship," Nugent said with assurance, "but will Belanger believe that she had been there all this time?"

"That I don't know," Barrow said. "All I know is that I want Marie discovered on the battleship and I want her to tell her father that she made the trip out of Nouméa on it."

"I'll do it," Marie promised, "and Father will believe me."

"But there's still the chance that Belanger will be out here before sunset," Nugent pointed out. "What will we do with Marie if he shows up?"

"We'll have to keep him from inspecting the area," Barrow said. "I don't want him prowling around where he might see her."

"He has a weak spot," Marie said. "I know how you can keep him in one place."

"How?" Nugent asked eagerly.

"Get him to talk about General De Gaulle."

"What do you mean?" Barrow demanded impatiently.

"General De Gaulle is his hero, and if you mention De Gaulle to Father, he'll talk about him all night. He adores that beanpole," Marie confided. "He thinks he looks like De Gaulle, too."

"So?"

"If you want to make a friend for life," Marie advised, "just tell Father that his resemblance to De Gaulle is remarkable."

"And with such frail weapons wars are won," Barrow muttered as he stalked to his quarters.

Major Barrow was upset and worried. He was frustrated. He felt that he was not getting a fair shake. The general was holding him responsible for actions of the paratroopers which he had absolutely nothing to do with. Here he was, trying to do a good job as commander of the paratroopers, and Burgermeister was threatening a disgraceful return to the United States. Even the French general, seemed determined to terminate the major's career—just when things looked so promising.

Barrow's worry and frustration turned toward the paratroopers, and developed into fury. The shenanigans of the troopers were the cause of all his trouble—their utterly ridiculous meddling in politics, holding out prisoners and hiring a general's daughter to make beds. It seemed that they were in a conspiracy to destroy him. There was only one possible future course of action in dealing with the paratroopers. In self-defense, he must be a tyrant. He would be the Prussian.

"I'm going to run this battalion like a concentration camp," he swore. "Before they can kill my career, I'm going to break the hearts of these renegades. I'll make life a living hell until they settle down and become Marines again. And, if I can't do that, I'll go to the general and admit that they should be disbanded, or dishonorably discharged from the Marine Corps."

First Sergeant Maxwellington joined the major. "It's getting to be just like Grand Central Station around here," he said.

"Why do you say that?"

"We haven't had so many visitors in this camp since the last time the general handed out decorations."

"I don't know what you're talking about," Barrow said impatiently.

"General Belanger just pulled into the area," Maxwellington explained. "He's over in front of the mess tent, jumping around like a jack rabbit. When I saw the fire in his eyes, I was going to sound battle stations."

Barrow held onto the center pole of the tent for support. "General Belanger is here?" he gasped.

"Big as life and twice as ugly."

"Oh, Lord," Barrow cried. "And we haven't gotten his daughter out of the camp yet."

"Well, you'd better get her under cover but quick."

Barrow rushed out of the tent and then held onto the guy rails of the pyramidals to keep from falling. In a stunning panic, he realized that he must find Marie—*quick*.

"Crocker," he hissed at the corporal, who was just passing the command post, "where's Marie?"

"She's over in A Company, taking a shower."

"Oh, no!" After a terrible pause of indecision, the qualities of leadership which the major possessed came to the fore. "Maxwellington," he ordered, "break out Captain Nugent and entertain the French general until I can get his daughter hidden. Occupy his time."

"I'll try, sir."

"Welcome to Tontouta." Maxwellington hurried to greet the general, signaling Nugent as he passed the adjutant's tent. "Glad to have you aboard, sir."

Barrow, sneaking out the back of his tent, heard the Free French leader's furious demand, "Where is my daughter?"

Major Barrow sped through the tent rows to the showers in A Company.

"Marie," he whispered hoarsely over the sound of the water. "Come out here. I've got to hide you. Your father is here."

"Hand me my clothes," Marie said in panic. "I'm naked."

"You haven't got time to dress," Barrow insisted. "Wrap this around you." He tossed Marie her slip over the canvas shower wall. "Hurry."

Holding the thin slip against her, the pretty girl ran out of the showers and followed Barrow into the company street.

"Where are we going?" she cried.

"I don't know," Barrow groaned as he turned into another street. "Where your father isn't."

Following Barrow, the girl ran through the streets of B Company and then back into the area of A Company. They sped through C Company, then, spying Belanger and Nugent, cut back through B Company.

The military life of the camp came to a sudden and happy standstill as Marines abandoned their stations and duties to line the boardwalks. Bakers stopped baking and cooks stopped cooking, while clerks ceased typing and filing to mill into the streets. Prisoners streamed out of the brig to follow the guards who had left their posts. Classes were dismissed and drill exercises halted as the growing crowd raced for strategic positions from which to view the wonderful sight of the nude girl who was running after the panting major.

While everyone else was enjoying the scene, Barrow suffered increasingly through fear of being detected in such a compromising situation by the general and for inflicting such embarrassment on poor Marie. The throngs of cheering and grinning Marines only added to his misery. Those enlisted men of his, his thoughts raged, were certainly a big help in an emergency. He felt terribly alone.

He wished he had used his head. He could have been a man and faced General Belanger and told him that Marie was a guest of the battalion. He could have, and should have, been prepared to tell the truth. Instead, in cowardly panic, he had worsened the situation and caused this terrible thing to happen to the lovely girl. He'd never forgive himself for this. Marie, that friendly and cheerful girl, was not deserving of such foul and cruel treatment. He didn't care about himself any longer, but what he was doing to his guest was unforgivable. That poor, sweet and *beautiful* girl!

"Marie," he almost sobbed, "I'm awfully sorry."

"I'm cold," she answered.

Exhausted, Barrow staggered through the street in officers' country for the fourth time.

"Help," he gasped. "Here they come."

Belanger, Nugent and Maxwellington, entering the street, gave Barrow no time to retreat into another area. In final desperation, he dragged Marie into his own tent and shook some clothes out of his seabag into his foot locker.

"In here, quick," he hissed at Marie, holding the top of the seabag open. "Hurry, girl."

"I hear my father," Marie squealed.

Barrow averted his eyes as Marie, brushing against him, climbed into the canvas bag. The major pushed her head down until she was out of sight, and crammed her slip under his pillow; then he slipped out the back of the tent and circled around to welcome the general.

"I wish I was back in Washington," he panted to himself.

Mustering his courage and stamina, Barrow hurried to the side of his important guest. "Welcome to my camp,

General De Gaulle," he stammered. "I mean, General Belanger."

The anger in Belanger's face diminished and a look of happy surprise took its place.

"Many persons have mistaken me for General De Gaulle," he said, "so please do not apologize."

"Your resemblance to the general is remarkable," Barrow parroted Marie's instructions.

"I take that as a compliment."

"The whole world admires that great man," Barrow said with increasing emphasis as First Sergeant Maxwellington looked at him with alarm and concern. "He will go down in history as one of the era's great leaders."

"What's the matter with the major," Maxwellington whispered to Captain Nugent. "He's beginning to rave like a maniac."

"Strategy," Nugent cautioned the Top Kick.

"You are probably one of the most discerning Americans I have ever met," Belanger said thoughtfully to Barrow.

"Why, thank you, General," Barrow said modestly, "and what happy occasion brings you to Tontouta?"

"I understand that my daughter might have been brought here as a guest of your men," Belanger answered. "I was not informed and, consequently, I have worried."

"What makes you think that?"

"A signalman from the *Missouri* suggested that one of your men knows of her whereabouts."

"You must know what crude and untruthful people those Navy men are, General."

"That is true," Belanger concurred, thinking back to the episode of the binoculars and the remarks of the sailors who were viewing his wife. "But I still must satisfy myself that she is not here."

"Would you like to inspect my camp?"

"With your permission."

"Certainly, sir," the major agreed, confident that the general would not be so presumptuous as to search officers' country. "You're just like General De Gaulle. Thorough."

Major Barrow, General Belanger, Captain Nugent and First Sergeant Maxwellington shook down the battalion area without uncovering a clue of Marie, and it wasn't difficult for the nervous major to talk Belanger into abandoning the search. That was especially true as they approached the command section.

"It's beautiful," Belanger exclaimed.

Barrow followed the Frenchman's eye and agreed. The strategy was beautiful. Stretched from two tree trunks and shading the street was a banner boldly proclaiming, "General De Gaulle for President." Another banner read, "General De Gaulle is Les Most." But the third one touched Belanger most deeply: "General De Gaulle Looks Just Like General Belanger."

"The world is safe," Belanger shouted in salute, tears streaming down his cheeks. "We cannot lose."

"Captain Nugent," Barrow commanded, "while the general and I are enjoying a Stump Juice cocktail, I want every man in this organization turned out to look for Miss Belanger."

"Yes, sir. Right away, sir," Nugent responded. "And Corporal Crocker has delivered the Stump Juice to your tent in officers' country."

"Well, have him bring it to my office," Barrow ordered.

"Your tent would be fine," Belanger assured the major. "Not so much dust there."

"Oh, no!" Barrow said in panic. "My tent is in disarray."

"That's perfectly all right," Belanger said, leading the way to Barrow's tent. "No need for formality."

Captain Nugent, the major and General Belanger sat on the edge of Barrow's bunk and sipped the cocktails that Corporal Crocker had prepared.

"You generals have so many problems." Barrow continued to play on the vanity of the Frenchman, hoping to keep his attention diverted from the seabag in the center of the tent. "So many responsibilities."

"How true," Belanger concurred. "Between my daughter, General Burgermeister and the Vichy, I know no peace."

"War is hell," Barrow said understandingly.

"Yes," Belanger concurred, "and these drinks are very powerful. It seems to me that your seabag is breathing."

Barrow smiled sourly. "The tropics play unusual tricks."

"I've been in the tropics a long time," Belanger reminded the major. "Do you mind if I look into that seabag."

Barrow laughed weakly. "There's nothing in that seabag except my laundry."

"Your laundry is squirming," Belanger said in surprise.

"Orderly!" Barrow shouted. "Help! Get this laundry out of here."

The Marines in the area were thrown into confusion. If they picked up the seabag with Marie in it, they might drop it or force the girl through the top of it. They hesitated.

Captain Nugent was no help, either. "What's this?" he asked, pulling a slip out from under Barrow's pillow. "Women's underwear?"

Barrow turned white and snatched the slip from Nugent's hands. "Clothing for the underprivileged children of New Caledonia," he explained weakly to Belanger. "We are collecting clothing for the youngsters."

"Fine." Belanger beamed. "About time the Kanakas got out of those silly Mother Hubbards they've been wearing for the past hundred years."

In his agitation, Major Barrow tipped over the seabag, bringing General Belanger's attention back to it. A slight moan escaped from the canvas sack as it hit the tent deck. General Belanger got up to examine the strange object while Barrow stood in numb terror.

In front of the tent, Corporal Crocker threw an imperative glance at Sergeant Fogleman and the men in the tent adjoining Barrow's. One of them pulled the pin of a tear-gas grenade and then ran through the streets, screaming, "Gas! Gas!"

The contents of the grenade floated with the wind and encompassed the men in Major Barrow's tent. Blinded and coughing, the men staggered for the sides of the tent to escape into the fresh air. Nugent and Belanger, nearing the door, were bumped back into the lung-burning and eye-stinging gas by two Marines wearing gas masks.

"I think I heard a woman scream," Captain Nugent exclaimed in alarm.

"Impossible," Barrow choked from the other side of the tent. "It was the battalion cat."

"The Vichy have attacked!" General Belanger solved the mystery of the gas.

As Barrow was rubbing his smarting eyes, he thought he saw two gas-masked Marines push their way into the tent and lift the now positively struggling seabag and carry it to the street. In the haze of burning chemical mist, he also thought he saw a white form emerge from the seabag and run from the area while the rest of the battalion stared and cheered.

Hearing the cheers, Belanger soothed his tortured companions with his proclamation: "The paratroopers have routed the Vichy. We are saved."

The group reconvened in Major Barrow's office.

"I'm awfully sorry," the major apologized to his guest. "The men were having classes in chemical warfare and the gas grenade got away from them."

"Accidents will happen," Belanger said magnanimously. "I'm just thankful it wasn't chlorine gas."

By sunset, the tin of medical alcohol and grapefruit juice was consumed by the now close friends, who spent the remainder of the afternoon discussing the attributes of General De Gaulle. As an orderly assisted Belanger into his jeep, Major Barrow, holding up a palm tree, announced, "As of today, this post shall be known as Camp De Gaulle."

"Vive la Camp De Gaulle," Belanger shouted. "Vive les paratroopers."

As General Belanger left for Nouméa, an LST put out from the Naval landing outside the city and circled toward the bay where the *Big Mo* was riding at anchor. Standing by the Marine at the wheel, was the pretty French girl and leaning against the gunwales were two Marines with samurai swords and Japanese battle flags.

"Those Seabees turn out a very good sword," Corporal Martin said to Pfc. Howes.

"Yeah," Howes agreed. "They look almost as genuine as our Jap banners."

As they neared the battleship, Marie crouched down in the shadows of the bow of the LST, while the Marines prepared to board the *Big Mo*. The Marines offered the sailors on watch a ridiculous bargain for the treasure they carried, asking only fifty dollars for the paraphernalia they had presumably risked their lives to acquire. Absorbed in the wonderful equipment, the sailors did not see the girl as she scrambled aboard the ship and ran into the deep shadows under one of the sixteen-inch rifles.

Their business concluded, the Marines left the *Big Mo* and returned to New Caledonia.

"That's going to be a confused ship," Martin told Howes. "When they discover that girl on the deck, there'll be an Easter egg hunt all through the fleet."

"There'll be action," Howes confirmed. "And Major Barrow will flip when we bill him for three hundred dollars to cover the cost of that gear we practically gave to that swabby."

"He'll pay it out of the battalion fund."

"I suppose it's worth it to him. He wants to get along with that silly French general."

"Yeah. He's a worrier."

# 8.

Major Barrow overslept the next morning and awoke with a cruel hangover. He felt no better when his orderly told him that General Burgermeister was on the telephone, screaming for the major.

Barrow staggered to the phone, and even without picking it up, could hear Burgermeister shouting, "Get down here, Barrow. Get down here right away."

"Oh, Lord"—the major shuddered as he drove to Burgermeister's office—"he's found out about Marie Belanger."

But General Burgermeister was not concerned about so small a matter as Belanger's daughter. Something really serious had happened.

When Major Barrow entered the general's quarters, Burgermeister was standing in the hall, waiting for him. "Come on," the general ordered, pushing Barrow toward his jeep.

They drove around the corner to where the flag tower stood. Three uneasy-looking Marines stood at the foot of it, holding the colors. The bugler stood nearby, shifting from one foot to the other.

"Look," the general commanded, pointing toward the small platform near the top of the tower. A foot was sticking out over the platform, caught in the halyard.

There was a paratrooper's boot on the foot. Noticing the size of the boot, Barrow correctly assumed that it was on the foot of Private Sigmund Yankowitz.

Yankowitz looked down at the assembled Marines, groaned and returned to the prone position.

"What happened, General?" asked Barrow.

"It seems, Major Barrow," the general began in an ominous tone, "that one of the highly trained and rigidly disciplined young men of your command went on the town last night after consuming a quantity of Stump Juice. After an especially hilarious time, which involved several M.P.s and some of our French friends, who are no longer our friends, your hero decided to climb that tower. He fell asleep, and when he awoke, the false courage of the Stump Juice had worn off and now he is afraid to climb down."

"Well," Barrow alibied lamely, recalling Yankowitz' service record book, "he spent most of his life in a coal mine."

"Regardless," Burgermeister interrupted with fury, "this is the first time in my thirty years in the Marine Corps that I haven't seen the flag raised with sunup. In my book, this is the most serious breach of conduct ever perpetrated by your menagerie—and that covers a wide territory."

"Climb down, Yankowitz," Barrow commanded. "Look up and climb down."

Yankowitz peeked over the side of his platform and quickly withdrew his head. "Can't," he bellowed.

"Please, Yankowitz," Barrow pleaded.

"Can't."

"I'll promote you to Pfc.," the major promised.

"Can't," Yankowitz wailed.

"I'll have you locked up for the duration if you don't," Barrow threatened.

"Can't."

"Paratroopers are not supposed to be afraid of height," Barrow coaxed.

"Go away, Corporal," Yankowitz groaned.

"I command you to descend," Barrow shrieked, aware of the danger in Burgermeister's eyes. "Please."

Yankowitz was half crazed with fear and wouldn't even try.

General Belanger, his lovely daughter beside him, joined the confused and angry group.

"What happened?" Belanger asked cheerfully, watching as several Marines climbed up and down the tower, showing Yankowitz how easy it was. "The big Marine is shy?"

"Please," Barrow shouted at his private, ignoring the Frenchman. "Come down."

"He appears to be frightened," Marie observed.

"Will everybody stop being so helpful," Burgermeister raged. "This is a catastrophe."

"He sobered up on the tower," Barrow explained to Marie. "Now he can't come down."

Marie took Barrow aside and whispered to him. The major looked at her in happy surprise and admiration. "Take the jeep," he murmured to the girl.

While the general looked on in glum madness, Marie careened out of the tower area on her way to Tontouta, where she explained her mission to Captain Nugent. The captain called for Corporal Crocker and outlined the situation. Crocker hurried to his tent and returned with a large container, which he put in the jeep, and Marie roared back to the flag tower. Barrow took the container, tied it to a halyard and raised it to the stricken private.

"You are a very resourceful man," Burgermeister snarled at Barrow. "You might even act as your own defense at your court-martial."

The men on the ground relaxed while Ziggy sipped on the container of Stump Juice. In a half hour he was singing songs of the mines, dangling his feet over the tower platform. In another fifteen minutes he was swinging and swaying down the ladder, making his descent with one hand on the jug and the other on the ladder stirrups. He was grinning happily as he touched the ground.

"Another pint," Burgermeister observed in terrible passion, "and he could have flown."

The music sounded "Call to the Colors" and the Marines stood at attention as the flag was raised—with the exception of Yankowitz, who passed out in the middle of the ceremonies.

"And now will you accompany me?" Burgermeister asked the major as he started back toward his headquarters.

The officers who were gathering for the regular staff meeting stood respectfully aside as Burgermeister stormed into his office. But as soon as General Belanger —who went along with the two Marines—saw Admiral Dorsey, he eclipsed even Burgermeister's nasty mood.

"You glorified deck ape," Belanger screamed at the American admiral. "You latter-day Captain Kidd."

"It's impossible that the girl could have been standing under that sixteen-inch rifle for two days without anyone seeing her," Admiral Dorsey protested, covering ground which the two men had, apparently, gone over before.

"You'd better check to make sure your engine rooms

aren't full of Japs," Burgermeister sneered at the Navy man.

"And my daughter does not lie," Belanger belabored the admiral.

"All right," Dorsey conceded. "She was found aboard my ship. I'll restrict every sailor on the *Missouri* until I find the man who took her aboard. But it still seems like a Marine trick to me."

"Marines have their faults," Major Barrow spoke up, "but they don't go around kidnapping young ladies."

"According to one of my signalmen," Dorsey thundered, "it is not beyond the realm of possibility that your beloved parachutists might know more than a little about this, Barrow."

"The men of Major Barrow's command are intelligent and honorable," General Belanger shouted at Admiral Dorsey.

"For a minute I thought I heard you siding with Major Barrow," General Burgermeister said to the man who had threatened to negotiate a separate peace with the Japanese because of the troopers.

"You did," Belanger confirmed. "If you had a few more officers like Major Barrow, we'd all be in Tokyo by now."

For the first time since the paratroopers had landed in New Caledonia, the unbelieving General Burgermeister saw a chance of cultivating amicable relations between the Americans and French. "I was thinking of appointing Major Barrow as liaison between your office and mine, General Belanger . . ." Burgermeister tested the ground.

"I was going to request it," Belanger agreed. "Major

Barrow is the only co-operative officer of your command."

General Burgermeister had completely lost the train of thought and could not possibly imagine what Barrow might have done to make the Frenchman feel kindly toward him, but wisely decided not to ask any questions. There are times, he thought, when what one doesn't know won't hurt one.

"My daughter expresses a desire to accept an invitation of your men to visit Tontouta," Belanger told Barrow. "After associating with sailors, I think that might be a good idea."

"That would be nice."

"She has implied that she and your battalion have a mutual commitment."

"Yes," Barrow said feelingly. "To win the war."

Admiral Dorsey did not take kindly to the reference made to his sailors. "I just might lay off this island," he muttered, "and rake your people with a few salvos."

"And Major Barrow and his paratroopers will sink your battlewagons," Belanger threatened.

Dorsey, who had heard much about the paratroopers and nothing good, decided not to push the matter.

"I'll see you in Tokyo," he said. "Before then would be much too soon."

He left, followed by General Belanger, who as he went out asked Major Barrow, "Will you escort Marie to Tontouta?"

"It would be a pleasure, sir," Barrow answered, and immediately realized that it would be, indeed, a pleasure to have the lovely girl as his guest. "I hope she will be able to stay a long time."

"I'm beginning to see you in a new light," Burgermeister said to Barrow when they were alone. "You might end up on the Joint Chiefs of Staff."

"Thank you, sir."

"Or Portsmouth Naval Prison."

"I was going to ask you to lift the restriction on the paratroopers and allow them to have liberty in Nouméa."

"No," Burgermeister said firmly. "Not now nor any other time."

"But Tontouta is so confining and there is so little to do there."

"I don't care. I love the simple people of Nouméa and I value the good will of General Belanger. No."

After the disappointed major left the office, Colonel Ward entered to deliver more bad news to the general.

"He arrives at the end of the week," Ward announced. "He left San Francisco yesterday."

"Who?" Burgermeister wanted to know.

"United States Senator John Patterson, Chairman of the Armed Forces Committee," Ward reminded the general. "He's coming out here to snoop on you and your command."

"That political hack," Burgermeister grunted. "Why doesn't he stay in Washington where he belongs. I've got enough problems without being that politician's caddy."

"You'd better be nice to him," Ward warned. "Remember, he handles appropriations and passes on promotions."

"I don't care," Burgermeister snarled. "Come VJ Day, I'm going to retire."

"In the meantime," Ward cautioned the general, "be very nice to the senator."

"I'll be as nice as I can to the windbag."

"All you have to do is give him a Cook's Tour of the island."

"All right," Burgermeister agreed. "I'll let him inspect the troops."

"With the exception of the First Parachute Battalion, of course," Ward added wisely.

"Naturally," Burgermeister agreed. "With the exception of the First Parachute Battalion. If Patterson ever visited that camp and found Japanese houseboys, it would stop my career like a ten-ton truck."

On the trip back to Tontouta, with Marie beside him in the jeep, Barrow recalled the events of the past day and a half. "I don't blame the general," he conceded. "The way they act, those paratroopers aren't safe to have around—even on this rock."

"You'll mold them into a fine battalion," Marie assured him.

"Thanks, Marie."

The nearness of the general's daughter caused him to remember with burning shame his awful tour of the battalion area, followed by the girl in her nakedness.

"You haven't been very well used," he apologized to Marie, "and I'm very sorry."

"You haven't heard me complain."

"No, I haven't. But walking you through the streets that way and pushing you into a seabag . . ."

"And gassing me." She giggled.

"It was terrible."

"I think it bothers you more than it does me."

"Maybe. It's just that I want you to know how much I regret that it happened."

"I know what you mean and I'm glad you feel that way. You're embarrassed for me."

"Yes."

"It's thoughtful of you to be so concerned for me."

"And I want to thank you for helping me get Yankowitz down from the flag tower." Barrow changed the subject. "That was clever thinking on your part."

"It was logical."

The very thought of Yankowitz on the tower and the towering rage of General Burgermeister, and the abuse he had taken, reawakened Barrow's anger toward his men. He renewed the vow he had made the previous night. "I'll snap them out of their hellishness," he ardently promised himself as he maneuvered the jeep along the twisting road, "or I'll drive the rest of them over the hill."

# 9.

If the paratroopers had cause to whine and complain because of Barrow's treatment of them the past few weeks, they screamed in anguish at the intensified program he proceeded to lay out for them. He put them on a more severe schedule than they had known even on Parris Island, where they had taken their initial training, and old-timers in the battalion could not remember a tougher taskmaster.

The men were up before dawn, doing close-order drill in platoon formation, running two miles through New Caledonian scrub before breakfast, taking lunch—with their backs against trees—in the middle of long hikes, falling exhausted into their bunks at night.

"This is worse than the training we got at the Lakehurst parachute school," Pfc. Howes complained bitterly.

"Much," Private Lincoln agreed. "We ought to make a deal with the Japs."

"They couldn't treat us any worse than Barrow," Sergeant Fogleman said seriously. "I think I'm beginning to like Japs."

"Me, too," Corporal Crocker agreed. "He's taking all the pleasure out of this war."

Even Marie expressed concern over the conditions in Tontouta.

"What are you doing to your men?" she asked the major, her eyes troubled for him. "They're getting blisters on their blisters."

"I'm trying to do a job," Barrow answered.

"They are very unhappy," the girl said sadly. "They think you hate them."

"Of course I don't hate them," Barrow assured her. "I have a great affection for them. But what I am doing is necessary."

"I suppose so," she acknowledged. "And I know you don't hate them, but I wish they liked you, too."

Captain Nugent approached the subject from a different angle. "You know these men have been in tough action," he told the major one day. "You can't give them a diet of that old stateside chicken stuff. They can't digest it any more. Every one of them has come within a hair's-breadth of being killed and they've buried a lot of their buddies. Why don't you treat them like Marines instead of recruits?"

"As commanding officer," Barrow defended himself, "I can't let them turn this area back into a pirates' camp. All I ask is that they conduct themselves like Marines instead of dead-end kids."

"Barrow's Boot Camp," Nugent said glumly. "This outfit is the joke of the Pacific."

"I'm sorry to hear that."

"Can't you mix a little kindness in with your discipline?" Nugent demanded. "Can't you meet them part way?"

Barrow thought this over. "Of course," he said, softening, "I should. They're doing a good job and I should reward them."

"How?"

"A beer party," Barrow planned happily. "Friday night I'll draw a supply of beer and we'll have a party."

Nugent wasn't so sure. "It sounds like a bribe," he said. "You are well on the way toward losing these men, and you can't buy them back for a bottle of Pabst."

"What would you suggest?" Barrow snapped, his happiness fading.

"There's one thing I'd like to bring to your attention."

"Certainly, what?"

Nugent crossed to the files and took out a report, its edges beginning to turn yellow. "Glance at this sometime when you have a few minutes," he suggested. "It might tell you more about the Marine Corps than you'll find in the Book you're trying to apply to this outfit."

In his tent, later that day, Barrow studied the report which Captain Nugent had given him. Sitting on his bunk, depressed, the skipper of the parachutists sadly examined the colorless and formal communication made out by a man who had led the troopers before him.

> *To:* The Commanding General
> *From:* C.O., 1st ParaBn.
> *Subject:* Casualties . . .

Down the length of the list—in its cold, alphabetical order—Barrow read the roll of the dead: the cruel, seeming endless tally of men who had gone into action with the battalion but who had remained forever on the islands and in the jungles and coconut groves of the British Solomon Islands, victims of the Japanese, statistics of desperately fought and hard-won battles. These were the men who would eternally carry the torch of American liberty, the men who made, and proved, America great. And the sorrowful major realized that the only difference between these dead heroes and his living scamps was the accident of Japanese marksmanship. If these boys had been left to live, on this day they would probably be driving stolen jeeps to steal the Navy's alcohol, be writing insolent additions to the Hymn of the organization they truly loved and believed in, laughing at rank and discipline they had found to be peacetime props of pompous unimportance. They would unconcernedly hand their machine guns to their prisoner buddies while they frolicked in the river. This was the other half of the First Parachute Battalion, parachutists forever.

In the somber and sobering list, Barrow knew, rested the solution to the problems he faced as the commanding officer of the survivors of the original battalion. And he realized the solution would never be fully known to him. Not having shared the terrible days of the first offensives —when the enemy was strong and experienced, these boys only half prepared and unskilled in their awesome profession—he could never completely understand the time and circumstances which had reshaped the characters of his men, who had been tempered in that fury.

He acknowledged he was a failure. And, as a failure, he could not retain a command he could not handle. Maybe another man would be more successful, an officer who knew of Gavutus and Bloody Ridges and the searing pain of 6.5s exploding from Japanese dugouts.

The paratroopers deserved such a man—the best one the Marine Corps could locate.

He had done it all wrong and he was sorry. He felt bad because he was a personal failure and would never realize the bright prospects General Burgermeister had held out as reward for a job well done. And he felt worse because he had developed a sincere affection for his high-spirited hellions, whom he really admired for their brash attitude and fantastic war record. He knew that his only honorable course would be to make out a report, outlining his decision, to General Burgermeister, telling him that, regrettably, he would not now have this battalion on the next push. He resigned himself to life in the auditor's office of the paymaster's department on the forgotten list. His combat career had been so short.

First Sergeant Maxwellington glanced into the tent, noted the tear-stained cheeks of the major, and entered to try to cheer up his commanding officer.

"You seem distraught," Maxwellington observed. "Why don't you go to the Fijis with me this week end?"

Barrow looked up at the Top. "For a second I thought I heard you say Fiji."

"I did," Maxwellington confirmed. "Pfc. Checkoway has some kind of a deal on with SCAT, and he flies a party to Suva every week end. He has a contract with a hotel and conducts a tour of the island with all the trimmings. Even a poi by firelight, with singers and dancers. It's out of this world."

"Who flies the plane?"

"Checkoway. He's getting pretty good. The pilots at Tontouta have been giving him lessons," Maxwellington explained. "They figure he'd steal the planes, anyway, and this way they're ahead of the game. They go out of their way to have a plane standing by for him every Friday night. Besides, he gives the pilots twenty-five percent of his take."

"That's thoughtful of him," Barrow said with sarcasm.

"It sure is," Maxwellington said, "especially when you consider the tour costs a hundred dollars and Checkoway carries about twenty people on his Happy Holiday Tour to the Fijis."

"Well, thanks anyway," Barrow declined the invitation. "I have neither the time nor the inclination to take such a trip."

Captain Nugent entered the tent and stood in awkward embarrassment.

"Yes, Captain?" Barrow looked up at his adjutant.

"About your beer party, sir," Nugent began.

"Oh," Barrow brightened. "Did you extend the invitation to all the men?"

"Yes, sir."

"What did they say," the major asked eagerly.

"Well, sir"—Nugent studied the floor, refusing to look his skipper in the eyes—"they weren't too enthusiastic."

"You mean they refused."

"Yes, sir. They refused."

"I see."

"I'm sorry, Major."

"Thanks."

Alone again in his tent, Barrow held the casualty list, the names of the heroes blurred by his tears. He put the document aside and placed a clean sheet of official stationery on his foot locker and began a letter to General Burgermeister.

> *To:* The Commanding General
> *From:* C.O., 1st ParaBn.
> *Subject:* Resignation . . .
> It is with the deepest regret that I tender my resignation as commanding officer, First Parachute Battalion, First Division . . .

# 10.

Before Major Barrow could send the memo to Nouméa, outlining his reluctant decision, General Burgermeister sent him the official communiqué which launched the affair of Kathy Kennedy, which in turn ended in an explosion that rocked, not only the island of New Caledonia, but Broadway, Hollywood, and Washington, D. C.

Major Barrow was so furious that he was actually frothing at the mouth after he read the bulletin handed to him by Captain Nugent, who met him in front of the adjutant's tent as he slowly walked toward his office. It was addressed to all commands and read in part:

> *Kathy Kennedy will entertain the troops stationed on this island tomorrow evening in the Pieta area. All officers and enlisted men are invited to attend the entertainment, with the exception of the First Parachute Battalion, First MarDiv.*

"Now, what in hell could have inspired a message like that?" Barrow demanded of Captain Nugent as he hammered the memo to the bulletin board in front of the armorer's tent.

"Well," Nugent tried to explain, "at the last couple of U.S.O. shows the men didn't exactly appreciate some of the acts or the music, and they stopped the show."

"How?"

"I guess you could call it a kind of riot."

"That's no excuse for embarrassing me and this organization in such a way," Barrow shouted, his eyes blazing.

"You got a case," Nugent agreed. "Don't blame me."

A few of the paratroopers came up to read the message on the board, and the word spread like a prairie fire in the wind. In seconds, the air was filled with screams of anguish and curses. Working parties disbanded, classes broke up, troop and drill was abandoned, and guards deserted the brig as the men raced for the bulletin board to see if the horrible news was true. A stunned silence followed the reading of the ugly document. They didn't believe it. They couldn't believe it.

"And that, for me," Corporal Crocker stated unequivocally, "is the end of World War Two."

"Well," Barrow—who had not moved since posting the bad news—shouted at the crowd of parachutists, "what are you going to do about that?"

"Any suggestions, Major?" Captain Nugent asked on behalf of the men.

The major's eyes swept the angry group of men around him. "I admit that you men have better imaginations than I, so I have no suggestions. But something is going to be done. Something had better be done. Or I'll lead this battalion on Pieta and wreck the joint."

A cheer went up from the men, and, in surprise, Major Barrow realized that the ovation was partly for him.

Mostly, of course, it was in anticipation of seeing the lovely Miss Kennedy.

"Well, let's think of something."

The men returned to their tents and talked in excited whispers. Plan after plan was discussed and discarded, and candles burned until long into the night. No one turned out for troop and drill in the morning, and the parleys went on. The problem was finally resolved.

Late in the afternoon the U.S.S. *America* pulled into the dock in the harbor of Nouméa. In addition to carrying replacements for the Army units on New Caledonia, the *America* had as her star passenger the beautiful Kathy Kennedy, rage of the barracks and the thing voted most worth fighting for by the combined forces. Accompanying her was a ten-piece all-girl orchestra, and lesser attractions, including comedians and singers. There was a large delegation to greet her, and a holiday mood prevailed over the otherwise gloomy Port of the Rock.

Miss Kennedy appeared at the head of the gangway and posed for the service photographers. The "ohs" and "ahs" that went up were genuine and spontaneous. Kathy was beautiful beyond description, from the top of her golden hair to her provocative ankles. Her blue eyes made prisoners of all the troops on the waterfront, and her half-parted lips captured every heart on the quay-side. To withhold this from the paratroopers was cruel and unusual, gave aid and comfort to the enemy, left no meaning to the war, and courted disaster.

"Hello, men," the actress breathed. "How are my heroes?"

"I'm dead," a sailor said as he swooned.

"I live," a Marine captain sighed as he passed out.

"If she had a sister," a soldier said, "I'd fight twice as hard."

"And I don't ever want to go home," a homesick Coast Guard bosun said, "as long as she hangs around this theater."

"God," another man put in, "I'm glad she wasn't at Pearl Harbor the day the Nips hit."

"Yeah," a full colonel added. "You'd think the government would have enough sense to tote her around in an armored truck."

"I know a guy who knows a guy who knows a friend of hers," a Navy commander bragged.

"I have seen her in person," a seaman second eclipsed that, staring at the luscious girl. "I am ready to die now."

A young and immaculate lieutenant stepped in front of the gathering crowd and introduced himself.

"I'm Lieutenant Johansen, General Burgermeister's recreation officer," he said gravely to the actress. "I'm to escort you to his quarters for cocktails before your show." He offered the lovely girl his arm and escorted her to the jeep he had standing by to take her to the Marine commander.

"To *the* General Burgermeister?" she said, thrilled.

"That's right, Miss Kennedy."

The lieutenant was very proud of his responsibility but was crestfallen when another jeep roared up alongside his, the red and gold flag and two stars of a major general flying from its fender. A major was sitting in the driver's seat.

"Not so fast," the major shouted at the lieutenant. "Get out of that jeep."

The major exchanged a hurried salute with the lieutenant and handed him a written message on General Burgermeister's letterhead.

"I'm Major Smithwycke from Intelligence, Lieutenant," the major explained, sweeping the waterfront suspiciously with his eyes. "Have you noticed any strangers around here?"

"Why, no, sir," the puzzled junior officer answered. "Is anything wrong?"

"Let me ask the questions, Lieutenant."

"Yes, sir."

"Did you send out the bulletin announcing that Miss Kennedy would entertain the troops in the Pieta area?" There was a strong tone of threat in the major's voice.

"Yes, sir. General Burgermeister told me . . ."

"Told you to advise every enemy agent in the Pacific theater where she'd be so they could murder the actress?"

"Oh, no, sir. That was not my idea at all."

"We'll discuss it further at your court-martial." The Intelligence officer scowled.

"At my court-martial?"

"Yes. In the meantime, because of your stupidity, the general has decided that it is now too dangerous to permit Miss Kennedy to perform in the Pieta area."

"What have I done?"

"The show must go on," Miss Kennedy said dramatically, moving away from the lieutenant who had exposed her to death, "even if I have to die."

"I'm to escort Miss Kennedy to Dumbea," the major said authoritatively. "You, Lieutenant, are to arrange transportation for the other entertainers."

"But, Major," the lieutenant protested, "General Burgermeister told me . . ."

"How long have you been in the Marines, Lieutenant?"

"Almost a year, sir."

"Hasn't anyone ever told you that you must obey orders promptly and cheerfully?"

"Yes, sir."

"Apparently you weren't impressed." The major was very angry. "You will answer to insubordination as well as the other charges against you at your court-martial."

"Please, sir . . ."

"Get these people off the waterfront," the major shouted in rage, "before your Vichy friends shoot them."

"I guess I won't have so much to tell my grandchildren after all," the lieutenant sighed as he took a last lingering look at Kathy Kennedy and turned to herd the other entertainers into the trucks.

Major Smithwycke helped the actress into the seat beside him. "Get in here quick, honey," he said, "before those sailors bite you."

Kathy got into the jeep. "This is exciting," she said.

"I feel like I've been shot from guns," Corporal Martin, masquerading as a major, said. "How about you and me finding a deserted island somewhere?"

"The Japs have all the islands." She giggled.

"I'll clean one up," Martin promised.

"Maybe after the war," the actress teased.

The phony major got his jeep back on the road, sped around the corner, passed the Banque d'Indochine and proceeded on the road toward Dumbea. They passed the Dumbea area but didn't even slow down. Finally the jeep pulled up at the area designated as Tontouta, land of the paratroopers; they had rigged a giant sign over their main street, which read, in letters two feet tall: "Welcome, Kathy Kennedy. We love you."

"She's here! She's here!" The shout went up from

the lusty-lunged paratroopers who had been biting their fingernails in anticipation of America's new sweetheart. "Martin did it!"

"Wow!" Lieutenant Chesley finally spoke to Captain Butts.

"Yeah," Captain Butts agreed.

"She's real," Corporal Crocker gasped to Pfc. Howes. "It wasn't just a bunch of propaganda to sell War Bonds."

"She's well and in good health," Pfc. Howes said studiously. "I don't understand why the war keeps going on."

The noisy welcome accorded Kathy aroused Major Barrow, who was sleeping in his tent. He hurried to the battalion streets to see what the commotion was all about, and immediately recognized Kathy Kennedy.

Noting the happy faces of his men, who had been so gloomy only a few hours before, he beamed gratefully on the adored actress who had come to visit his area.

"Miss Kennedy"—he saluted the girl—"it was so nice of you to come to Ton . . ."

Martin hurried Miss Kennedy over to him and, before Barrow could finish his greeting, said, "Kathy honey, I would like you to meet General Burgermeister." He nodded toward Major Barrow.

"What are you talking about, Martin?" Barrow whispered.

"I'm so happy to meet you, General Burgermeister," the girl said and offered Barrow her hand. "I've heard so much about you. You've been my hero ever since the war started."

"Of course," the overwhelmed Barrow stammered. "Well, let's all have a drink."

Several of the men dashed for their tents. In a few

seconds, Barrow could hear the rumble of five-gallon tins. Soon the Marines were back with buckets of Stump Juice, canteen cups of which were handed Miss Kennedy, the major, and all the officers and men of the battalion.

"It's delicious, General," Kathy exclaimed. "You must give me the recipe."

"Sure, doll," Corporal Crocker spoke up, "five gallons of medical alcohol and a quart of grapefruit juice. Serve in a well-chilled canteen cup. It's got to have that flavor of aluminum to be any good."

"Give her a mess kit and we'll have some chow," the cook bellowed. "Spam à la Kennedy."

Miss Kennedy and the officers and men all ate in the enlisted men's mess tent, standing at the boards that lined the tent. There were no chairs and tables. The Spam and dehydrated cabbage tasted so good, with Miss Kennedy a guest, that for the first time in three months the cook escaped being promised a beating.

"It's delicious," Kathy exclaimed.

"She must be in a state of shock," Private Lincoln muttered.

"Aw, really, Kathy"—the cook blushed—"it stinks but it's all we got."

"If she says it's delicious, it's delicious, you baker with his brains baked out," the men began to shout.

Sensing catastrophe, Major Barrow, whom Miss Kennedy persisted in calling General Burgermeister, suggested that they leave the crowded mess tent and start the entertainment in the broad company streets.

"That's what I'm here for," Miss Kennedy announced. "To help you men forget the war for a few minutes."

"What war?" the starry-eyed paratroopers wanted to know.

"But my music isn't here," Miss Kennedy suddenly remembered.

"Think nothing of it, dearie," First Sergeant Maxwellington surprised the battalion by stating, "I am the best harmonica player this side of Borrah Minnevitch."

"You're terrific, Sergeant, but I can't help wondering what happened to my all-girl orchestra."

"The officers probably got them," Private Lincoln said. "You'll never see them again."

"Well"—Kathy shrugged—"let's make music."

Accompanied by the Scotsman, who amazed the troopers by his ability to wring music out of the harmonica which had been hidden in his desk since he joined the Marine Corps, Kathy serenaded the warriors. To the men, her voice was that of an angel.

"Gee, that was beautiful, Kathy," Corporal Crocker said as she finished her first number. "What was the name of it?"

"That was 'The Star-Spangled Banner,'" she said, surprised.

"It will be a great hit," Crocker predicted.

"Do you dance, General?" the starlet breathed at the major, as First Sergeant Maxwellington entertained with a solo.

"You only go this way once," the newly promoted general told himself as he whirled the beautiful blonde through a waltz.

Between dances, Kathy expressed concern over the other troops on the island. "I can't understand where they are," the visitor said. "There were supposed to be thousands of men here."

"That's the history of this rock, doll," she was told. "Always a foul-up somewhere."

"But you didn't foul-up on Guadalcanal, did you, General?" Kathy asked the major, worshipping him with her large blue eyes.

He blushed modestly, and then whispered to Captain Nugent, "Let me borrow a few of your campaign bars, will you?"

"Anyone you want except my Good Conduct medal," Nugent replied.

And then the cry came down from the lookouts who were watching the road to Nouméa. The dread cry: "Here they come. Here they come. Hide the merchandise."

The major's insignia came off Martin's shoulders and were tucked into his back pocket. The sign of greeting that hung over the company street was torn down and hidden in the tub of dehydrated cabbage. The general's flag was ripped off the fender of the jeep and stuffed into the gas tank. The Stump Juice was whipped into the tent of the bartender.

"What are we going to do with her?" the major screamed in panic, pointing toward the actress.

Private Polk, the morale officer's assistant, ran up to the major. "Put her in a seabag. Put her in a seabag."

"Shut up."

"We'll wrap her in sheets and bury her," Corporal Martin offered. "We'll give her a straw to breathe through."

"I could put Kathy into one of my pots," the cook volunteered, "but I couldn't get her in in one piece."

"Hey," Crocker exclaimed, "the cook's got a good idea. Come on." He grabbed one of his buddies and ran into the woods behind the tent area, returning in seconds with the largest pot the major had ever seen.

"What's that?"

"I use it for distilling aniseed. The Navy Construction Battalion made it for me," Crocker said.

Miss Kennedy was becoming alarmed. The agitated conversations and conduct of the men unnerved her.

"What's the matter, General?" she pleaded. "What happened?"

"Hill bandits," Major Barrow answered. "They're going to attack the camp. Terrible people. We've got to hide you."

"Give me a rifle," she suggested. "I'll defend myself."

"Couldn't think of it. Against our code of honor."

Unceremoniously, America's sweetheart was dumped into the vat used for making bootleg anisette and dragged behind the galley, where the cook sat on the lid.

Miss Kennedy was no more than out of sight when a jeep carrying General Burgermeister roared into the area. With him was an impressive civilian, obviously a *Very Important Person*. Before the vehicle stopped, Burgermeister leaped out and charged up to Major Barrow.

"Where is she?" Burgermeister screamed, his face nearly purple with rage. "Where? Where? Where?" He paused and glanced around the area at the faces viewing him in feigned surprise.

"I'll send you to Portsmouth for this, Barrow. I'll have you executed. Where is she?" The famed Burgermeister voice was booming full blast.

"Who?" the major asked in wide-eyed innocence.

"Kathy Kennedy, that's who." The general was nearly out of his mind.

"We wouldn't know, General," Major Barrow said stiffly. "We weren't invited to her performance."

"Please, Major"—the general, deflated, began to plead —"if you know where she is, just tell me and we'll forget the whole thing."

"Don't know nothing," the major said smugly.

"I'll see that you get a promotion," the general said.

"Sorry. I can't help you." Barrow knew that the general would skin him alive once he got the actress.

"My God," the civilian at Burgermeister's side shouted in alarm, "they're armed! They're all carrying weapons."

"Who?" The major, startled, looked toward the hills.

The civilian spun on General Burgermeister. "You told me this area was set aside as a concentration camp for your penal battalion. How is it you allow them to be armed?"

General Burgermeister was embarrassed and then alarmed when he saw the hostile look in the eyes of the paratroopers. Now the battalion knew why they had not been inspected by the distinguished United States senator who had visited all the other Marine camps.

Seeing the general's predicament—trapped in the lie he had devised for the senator, embarrassed before the paratroopers, and desperate to find the lost actress— Major Barrow decided to strike a blow for his men.

"I meant to ask you, General, if you would consent to having this battalion transferred to the States for retraining. They went through a lot in the Solomons and . . ."

But the general was not that desperate. "Are you out of your mind, Barrow? Send this pack of Indians back to the States? As a group? Have you lost all love for your native land?"

"Do you think it's safe for us to be here?" the civilian asked nervously.

"This is Senator Patterson," Burgermeister lamely introduced the two men. "And this is Major Barrow."

"How do you do, sir?"

The Marine general returned to the cause of his visit. "This is serious, Major," he said. "If anything happens to that girl, they'll hang me in front of the White House."

"What happened?" Barrow asked innocently.

"Some devil in paratrooper's boots, masquerading as a major from my Intelligence section, kidnapped her."

"It couldn't have been one of my men, General."

"Oh, no?" the general bleated. "Well, where are the major's insignia you're supposed to be wearing?"

The major's hands jumped to his shoulders, feeling for his gold leaves. They were gone, stolen by Martin while he slept.

"I don't go around pulling my rank on my men all the time, like some officers," he said weakly.

An approving cheer from the troopers drowned out the general's reply.

"Maybe you and your pack of con men and thieves didn't kidnap Miss Kennedy, Barrow. Personally, I think you did," Burgermeister said through clamped teeth, "and I'm going to find out. Fall the men out while I shake down the area."

"Yes, sir." Barrow nodded for Captain Nugent to comply with Burgermeister's order.

"My idiotic recreation officer is now scanning the picture of every man on this island," the general said, his voice dripping with malice. "Heaven help you and these men if he is able to identify one of your gangsters as the culprit."

"And heaven help you, too," the Chairman of the Armed Forces threatened General Burgermeister, "if you don't locate that actress. You'll be mowing lawns in Quantico until the Board of Review approves the findings of your court-martial."

Prancing in rage, General Burgermeister led the senator and the major on an inspection of the paratroopers' camp. In the other units the men had all fallen out together to be inspected, but United States Senator Patterson noticed that the paratroopers stayed in their tents, holding canteen cups, until the last possible minute in the tent-by-tent inspection. However, Patterson soon felt that he was looking over the finest troops in the division, and he told Burgermeister that. It served to keep the general's rage in check.

With Major Barrow and Senator Patterson on either side of him, Burgermeister hurried through the area, searching for the girl, glancing at the men. He wanted to find the missing actress and get Patterson out of Tontouta before something happened. He should have known better.

Among the men in front of a tent in C Company stood Private Yankowitz, every bit at attention and the picture of a perfect Marine. But when the inspection party approached his group, instead of holding his ground, Yankowitz advanced on the party and shouted at Major Barrow, while looking at the man in civilian clothes, "A friend of yours, Mac? Well, a friend of yours is a friend of mine." And Yankowitz extended his hand to Senator Patterson. "Just call me Ziggy."

The general turned blue and Barrow was too shocked to speak.

"A friend of yours, Mac," Burgermeister hissed

through his teeth. "You'll have a chance to make a whole new circle of friends."

Yankowitz had a wide grin on his face. He was telling the senator, whom he suspected of being a big wheel, "This guy, Corporal Barrow, is an ace-high straight flush. Best guy you ever met. We all love him."

"Please, Yankowitz . . ." Barrow muttered.

"Be my guest," Burgermeister growled at the private; then he called for his runner, and said, "Escort this bright young man to the First Guard Company. Tell them to put him up for a month—on bread and water."

"What did he do?" Patterson asked in surprise. "I think it's nice of the men to speak up for their commanding officer."

"It's all right," Burgermeister assured the senator, increasing his steps, hurrying up the inspection. "I should never have brought this man up here," he thought. "I should never have come up here myself."

Lagging behind, Senator Patterson shouted in excitement and joy, "I found her. I found her. Wow! What a lovely bundle."

Major Barrow felt his knees buckle and was grateful when General Burgermeister grabbed his arm to steady him. But the general was pushing and pulling him toward the tent where Senator Patterson was announcing his happy discovery.

On the floor of the morale officer's assistant's tent sprawled a lovely Javanese girl. All she was wearing was a smile.

"That's not Miss Kennedy," General Burgermeister shouted at the senator. "That's not Miss Kennedy at all."

"Who is she?" Patterson asked in wonder.

"She's an orphan," Barrow stammered. "The men put

her in there until they can accumulate clothing for her."

Burgermeister's jaw quivered as he looked down on the naked girl. "Barrow," he said in absolute awe, "this is the most incongruous thing I have ever seen in my entire tenure. A nude girl in a seabag in a Marine's tent. We'll build you a special dungeon in Portsmouth."

"I think it's thoughtful of Major Barrow to care for this poor little orphan," Patterson said, enjoying his view of the poor little orphan. "Commendable."

"Let's retire to your office," Burgermeister said grimly to Barrow. "We can start writing up specifications for your trial immediately."

As he rounded the corner of a company street, Burgermeister stopped short, seeing Marie Belanger busily spreading a blanket over the top of a Marine's bunk.

"Is that her?" Senator Patterson asked hopefully. "She certainly is beautiful enough to be a movie actress."

"That's our maid—our guest," Barrow stuttered.

"That's Marie Belanger," Burgermeister gasped. "In an enlisted man's bed."

"I am not in bed," Marie said haughtily. "I am merely making the bunk."

"What are you doing in this canvas bedroom?" Burgermeister was horrified. "If your father . . ."

"Father sent me here," Marie told the general.

"Such a cruel and unusual thing to do," Burgermeister whispered as he ran for Barrow's office.

They got to the office just in time for Burgermeister to accept a telephone call which had come in for him from Nouméa.

"It's the brig warden," First Sergeant Maxwellington told the general. "He's calling about Private Yankowitz."

"What does he want?" Burgermeister fumed.

"Yankowitz found in the prison rules that a prisoner on bread and water is entitled to have a Bible in his cell. He wants a Bible."

"Well," Burgermeister snarled, "give him a Bible."

"It's not quite that easy, sir," Maxwellington explained. "Yankowitz doesn't want just any old Bible."

"Are you trying to torment me?"

"No, sir. Yankowitz wants a special Bible."

"What's the matter with the regular Bible?" Burgermeister, never a patient man, was swelling in fury.

"Yankowitz has read it," Maxwellington said. "He thinks he'd like to read the Book of Mormon."

"Very well"—Burgermeister grimaced—"tell the brig warden to give that character the Book of Mormon."

"That poses a problem, too." Maxwellington faced the glaring general.

"Tell me why, please."

"The warden says he can't find a Book of Mormon. He's been all over the base and there isn't a Book of Mormon to be had. He has tried the skippers of the Fifth, First and Eleventh Regiments and nobody in those outfits has a Book of Mormon. He called the base quartermaster, and he doesn't even know how to go about requisitioning one. There's an Army chaplain up at the end of the island who has one, but he says it's none of his concern, and the Book of Mormon he has, he brought into the service with him."

"Enough!" Burgermeister roared. "Tell Yankowitz he can't have the Book of Mormon."

"But he can, sir. The Judge Advocate's office has ruled that 'Bible' is to be interpreted as the text of any organized and recognized religion."

"Is Yankowitz a Mormon?"

"No, sir."

"I fail to see why I should be subject to dilemmas such as this." Burgermeister was beside himself. "I'm a general. I was sent out here to plan vast maneuvers and win a hemispheric war. I'm too valuable to be persecuted this way."

"Yankowitz indicated that he'd settle for a copy of *Mutiny on the Bounty*," Maxwellington said apologetically.

"Thoughtful of him." Burgermeister glared at Maxwellington. "Tell the warden to give him *Mutiny on the Bounty*."

"There's a Seabee at Magenta who has a copy," Maxwellington went on. "He wants four dollars and fifty cents for it."

"Tell the warden to give the Seabee four dollars and fifty cents for it."

"The warden won't, sir. He isn't going to pay four dollars and fifty cents to buy Yankowitz reading material."

"Well, who is?"

"You, sir."

"All right. All right. I'll pay for it, but hang up that phone." The general looked grimly into space and then turned to Major Barrow. "How long ago was it that I sent Yankowitz to the brig?"

"Less than an hour ago, sir."

"Things happen fast where your men are concerned, Barrow." The general looked helplessly toward the senator. "I forget what I was going to say when I came into this tent, and before my headache gets any worse, I suggest we leave this place."

The general's jeep left the camp in a cloud of dust. First Sergeant Maxwellington roused the major, who had relapsed into a state of semishock. "He's gone. What do we do now?"

"Do about what?"

"The actress, Kathy Kennedy."

"We've got to get her out of this area," Barrow answered vaguely. "Bring her out here."

Miss Kennedy was let out of the vat and brought back into the center of the company street near the mess hall. "How did the battle go?" she asked, rubbing her back.

"We repulsed them," the major assured her.

"I didn't hear a shot fired," she said.

"Hand to hand. Bayonet work, miss. That's how we always fight them. They don't have rifles." The major was surprised at his own glibness.

"Oh, General, you're so gallant."

"We can't thank you enough for the marvelous entertainment, Miss Kennedy," Barrow told her. "It was wonderful and I'm sure there are other units waiting to hear you sing. I'll have you driven back to the city in a closed recon truck."

"Why a closed truck?"

"Just in case there are any snipers around."

"That will be exciting." Miss Kennedy was enjoying this candid look into the lives of her heroes. "And I've never enjoyed giving a performance as much as this one."

"You might have time for an encore, doll," said Sergeant Fogleman, in charge of lookouts.

Barrow looked up. "What now?" he asked with a sigh.

"They've set up a road block a half mile from here," Fogleman reported. "No traffic getting through without a shakedown."

"Who?" Kathy asked. "The hill bandits?"

"Of course," the sergeant told her.

"We've got to get this young lady to Nouméa." There was a note of desperation and pleading in Major Barrow's voice as he addressed this remark to the paratroopers.

"How?" a company clerk wanted to know. "There's only one road out of here."

"We'll go around the road, then." The major thought that was a good idea.

"Not with her, you won't," he was informed by Corporal Crocker. "There's hundreds of feet of cliff on one side and thick woods on the other. I don't think a rugged man could make it, let alone a sweet, adorable, lovely, luscious dream like Kathy."

"We'll build a raft and float her down the Dumbea River," Martin said. "We'll use sheets for sails."

"Smuggle her out in a seabag," suggested Private Polk.

"The river ain't more than two inches deep in some places and there are Army camps and hospitals all along it. And the M.P.s would open the seabag."

"We'd better lay low for a while until the heat's off," Maxwellington said. He disapproved of this business but he stuck with his outfit. "Let's sleep on the problem."

"Hey, the first sergeant's making jokes."

"That's the most sensible thing he ever said," Pfc. Howes told Corporal Martin as they admired the "problem."

But the men agreed. Kathy Kennedy was given the major's tent. Barrow moved in with Captains Nugent and Butts.

Candles burned late into the night and plans were exchanged from tent to tent, but in the morning the eyes of the troopers were not bright with schemes; they were haggard from lack of sleep and lack of plan. The M.P.s had cut them off more successfully than the Japanese Imperial Army had been able to do.

"Maybe we can keep the darling here until VJ Day," Howes offered hopefully.

"That would be nice," Martin agreed, "but we'll probably be sent on another strike before this war is over."

"So we got our own nurse," Fogleman observed. "The Japs take women along with them. Why shouldn't we?"

"You know the Japs are years ahead of us," Private Lincoln pointed out.

# 11.

For three days and three nights the men paced the decks of their pyramidals, bit their fingernails and pulled their hair, but found no way of circumventing the road block. They began to lose confidence in themselves, an experience they didn't believe possible.

And as they listened to the radio, they began to know fear. What had started as a vengeful joke had turned into an international situation of utmost gravity. The newscasts were ominous and frightful.

HOLLYWOOD: *"The motion picture industry has lost its most promising young star, Kathy Kennedy, who has been reported missing in the Pacific area. Her studio announced plans to do the story of her life in Technicolor, the gallant story of the first of filmdom to fall on the field of battle."*

NEW YORK: *"The Theater Group today announced plans to build a memorial in remembrance of the loveliest casualty of the war. A dignified shaft of white marble will stand near Forty-Second Street and Broadway, a silent reminder of the girl who lived life so much [the announcer's voice broke] that she was willing to die in what she considered to be a good cause."*

COMMENTATOR: *"Why haven't the details of Kathy Kennedy's disappearance been disclosed to the Ameri-*

can public who loved her? Who's covering up for whom?
How about it, Pentagon? How about it, White House?"

WHITE HOUSE: "We are doing all we can to uncover the
details of the supposed death of Miss Kennedy. In the
meantime, we look upon her demise as we do that of any
of our young people who have made the supreme sacri-
fice. She died in battle."

Kathy wept softly as she heard the sentimental bul-
letins. At other times she was overawed and overjoyed
at the publicity she was getting and, when she was sure
she was still alive, her face glowed with vanity and
happiness over the concern expressed by the world for
her.

"Boy, am I a celebrity," she squealed with delight.
"Me, in Technicolor. Gee!"

The enthusiasm and gaiety of the actress only further
accentuated the plight of the paratroopers. The longer
she stayed in their camp, the greater the chances of de-
tection became, and the sterner General Burgermeister's
punishment would be. At any time, Lieutenant Johansen,
General Burgermeister's recreation officer, might come
upon the service record picture of Corporal Martin, and
then the battalion would die.

With this in mind, the paratroopers racked their brains
to come up with the solution to their problem: that of
safely delivering the actress to Nouméa without being
identified with her kidnapping.

It was Private Lincoln who made the ominous an-
nouncement. "When we finally do get her out of here,
she's going to spill the whole story. So, actually, what
are we doing but postponing the execution?"

That did it. With a dull thud, the whole glorious bottom fell out.

Marie Belanger, sweating out the problem with her companions, finally came up with the solution.

"There must be a way for you men to get around that road block," she insisted.

"You tell us how, sweetface," Corporal Martin said, "and we'll write you up for the Legion of Merit."

"If you can't go around it, go over it," Marie suggested.

Major Barrow sighed in discouragement. "How can we go over the road block?" he wanted to know.

"You're parachutists, aren't you?" Marie pressed.

"Of course," the major answered.

"Well, what are parachutes for?"

"Huh?"

"Fly over the road block and jump."

It was as simple as that.

"Marie, you're wonderful," Barrow said. "You're the only man in this battalion with a head on his shoulders."

"What a man!" the paratroopers enthused.

But First Sergeant Maxwellington, always the realist, stuck a pin in the bubble. "We ain't got no planes and that actress is not a chute jumper."

The shoulders of the men slumped and their happy smiles faded.

But Marie was ahead of Maxwellington, too. "Pfc. Checkoway, the Charles Lindbergh of your battalion, has a standing requisition for planes," she pointed out, "and Sergeant Fogleman was an instructor at your parachute training school."

"She's right," Barrow exclaimed. "Fogleman could teach her a simple tumble . . ."

"So she wouldn't break her sweet, lovely, adorable neck when she lands," Corporal Martin added.

The enthusiasm was mounting to the boiling point when Private Lincoln threw another monkey wrench into the blossoming plans. "Better kill her and bury her. She'll expose us when she gets out of here. What's she going to tell people? Hill bandits?"

"Lincoln is right," Major Barrow said. "There's only one thing to do. Howes, get Miss Kennedy out here."

"My God, Major," First Sergeant Maxwellington gasped, "you're not going to murder that girl, are you?"

"Of course not."

The men sat in a semicircle on the company street and quizzically watched their commanding officer as he stood before them with the actress by his side.

"Miss Kennedy," he began, "there are no hill bandits. We kidnapped you."

"You did? Why?" She didn't know if the situation was funny or serious. She was perplexed.

"Read this." Major Barrow handed her a copy of the bulletin sent out from the general's office, prohibiting the paratroopers from sitting in on her show.

Kathy studied the bulletin and her brow wrinkled in confusion. "Why would the general send you such a nasty note?"

"Maybe he doesn't like us," Private Lincoln said. "But then, he doesn't like anyone."

"Well, I don't blame you for what you did," the girl said angrily. "It isn't democratic."

"Then you aren't angry at us?"

"Of course not." Her eyes became misty. "It's the greatest compliment I ever received in my life."

"It is?" Barrow said, marveling.

"We ought to compliment you more often," Martin said.

"To think," Kathy sighed, "you wanted to see me so badly that you went to all that trouble and ran that great a risk."

"We've run greater risks for much less," Pfc. Howes said modestly.

"It was the first risk I ever saw that was worth running," Martin said.

"You wanted to see me so much that you went so far as to kidnap me." Kathy was thrilled. "I'm overwhelmed and deeply grateful."

"Oh, Lord," Maxwellington groaned. "Every woman that comes to this island from now on is a dead cinch to be kidnapped."

"I'm glad you did it," Kathy announced emphatically.

"So are we." The men nodded.

"Right now, the important thing is getting you back. After this hoax, you can imagine what will happen to us. The President himself will shoot us."

The men thought the major was doing a good job, although somewhat melodramatic.

"Oh, no!" A realization struck Kathy which had escaped the paratroopers. "I'll be ruined. All that publicity. Killed in action. Technicolor. They'll think it was all a cheap gag, and I'll be the laughingstock of Hollywood."

"Then that puts us all in this thing together," Major Barrow said, "but if you'll go along with us, Kathy, everything will come out all right."

"You won't expose me?"

"Not if you don't expose us," Barrow answered.

"But what will I tell people?"

"Leave that to us. We'll think of something."

"Anything you say, fellows."

"How would you like to make a parachute jump, Miss Kennedy?" Barrow asked as the men leaned forward tensely to catch her answer.

"I'd love to. That would be exciting."

As the men came to attention before their gallant lady, Major Barrow stepped forward to pin a set of paratrooper's wings on her blouse. Kathy closed her eyes in ecstasy. So, as a matter of fact, did Major Barrow. If his men heard his low whistle and noticed his crimson cheeks as he clumsily attached the pin to the actress' clothing, they gave no indication of it.

"You are hereby made an honorary member of the First Parachute Battalion, Inc.," he said with great feeling, "and your name shall be inscribed on the rolls of this organization forever."

The men applauded.

"Gee," Captain Nugent said, "wouldn't it be swell if she were a man so she could be a real paratrooper?"

First Sergeant Maxwellington watched the swaying hips of Kathy as she walked toward her tent. "You must be out of your head, sir. We never needed paratroopers that bad."

It was easy for Sergeant Fogleman to teach Kathy the rudiments of tumbling, the most important part of jumping, and the work was made especially easy because the beautiful actress and the wild men had come, in their brief time together, to love one another.

"Well," Sergeant Fogleman was able to report to

Major Barrow in a few days, "the girl can tumble. What are we going to do now? Put her in a plane and kick her out over Place des Cocotiers and let the M.P.s pick her up?"

"I suppose so," the major replied. "No one has thought of anything else."

"And there she shall stand," Marie spoke up, "draped in a parachute. General Burgermeister won't have much trouble figuring out where she got that gear."

"Haven't you thought of an alibi for me yet?" Kathy demanded of the men. "I've got to have a better story to tell than my last three movies had."

"We'll think of something," Corporal Crocker said.

But neither the Marines nor the girls were at all confident that a good enough idea would be hit upon.

"Why don't you slip her aboard the *Big Mo?*" The loud voice of Private Yankowitz joined the conversation. "That should send Admiral Dorsey home in a strait jacket."

"What are you doing around here?" Major Barrow snapped at the big Marine. "You're supposed to be in the First Guard Company's brig."

"They threw me out for creating a disturbance," Yankowitz explained. "I was dishonorably discharged from the brig."

"That shapes," Corporal Martin nodded his head. "What did you do?"

"Nothing." Yankowitz proclaimed his innocence. "The prison rules say that a prisoner on bread and water is entitled to as much water as he can drink and as much bread as he can eat. The bakers refused to work nights and threatened to strike."

"So you ate your way out of the brig?" Martin marveled. "I'll have to remember that."

"No," Yankowitz corrected, "they couldn't keep me fed. I love bread."

"Please leave this meeting," Barrow told the private. "We are trying to think."

"I have a good mind to resign my commission and quit this war," Yankowitz threatened.

"Your resignation is accepted," Barrow said impatiently.

The unwanted private left the tent and was joined by the unhappy actress, who believed her career was coming to an end because of the awful circumstances she found herself in.

"Did they throw you out of the tent, too?" Yankowitz asked her.

"No," Kathy answered. "They're trying to help me."

"Help you to do what?"

"Help me to get out of here and save my reputation."

"Which one of the men did it?"

"Did what?"

"Ruined your reputation."

"I don't understand what you are saying," the distraught actress answered. "I think you have lost me."

"I'll marry you," Yankowitz offered gallantly. "Your child can take my name."

"Thank you," the actress said in confusion. "That's thoughtful of you."

"Any time," said the expansive Yankowitz.

"And I have gotten all those wonderful men in trouble." Kathy wept.

"Impossible," Yankowitz exclaimed in amazement. "Now you have lost me."

"They wanted me to be their guest and brought me up here without telling General Burgermeister," Kathy reminded Yankowitz, "and now they can't get rid of me without getting into terrible trouble. The general will kill them."

"It's all a war of nerves," Yankowitz said sagely. "Everybody's against everybody else. I wish I had never come up out of the mines."

"My father was a miner," Kathy answered absently. "I was brought up in a mining town."

"A Pennsylvania coal miner?" Yankowitz asked eagerly.

"No. Colorado copper," Kathy answered.

"Too bad this island doesn't have coal," Yankowitz began to talk intelligently. "I never saw such iron deposits. With coal, New Caledonia could have the biggest steel mills in the world."

"Imagine that," Kathy said, losing interest. "Steel mills."

"I can show you some hills that run more than fifty-five percent iron," Yankowitz boasted. "Want to see them?"

"We can't leave here," Kathy said. "There's a road block only a half mile from here."

"That's on the road to Nouméa," Yankowitz pointed out. "The iron hills are in the other direction—up-island."

"How far are these deposits?" Kathy's interest was re-awakened by Yankowitz' words and her own thoughts.

"At least fifty miles, I guess."

"Can you take me there right now?"

"Sure."

"I'd like to go, then."

"Now?"

"Right now."

"Okay."

While the battalion planned Kathy's cover story, she took a ride into the wild and upper regions of New Caledonia with the private. After passing the communities of Boulouparis, La Foa, and Moindou, the Marine turned at Bourail and headed for the heart of the Chaine Centrale.

Finally Yankowitz stopped the jeep in a Kanaka village, where the natives happily and affectionately greeted him. The Marine then walked the actress to the mines where the wealth of New Caledonia was being probed by native laborers.

"Isn't that beautiful?" he asked Kathy.

But Kathy was not concentrating on the reddish soil of the mineral deposits. She kept glancing over her shoulder at the fierce-looking Kanakas who had followed her and the Marine from the village. Most of the New Caledonians were carrying long knives. Huge black men with fuzzy hair died orange with lice-killing lime, they studied the American blond in utter fascination.

"Yankowitz," she finally cried. "Will these natives harm us?"

"No." Yankowitz laughed. "They think I'm crazy."

"I don't get the connection."

"They think crazy people are sacred," Yankowitz informed her. "They treat them like gods, bring them gifts of fruit and other things."

"One of them is bringing me a big sweet potato," Kathy said in alarm. "Do they think I'm crazy, too?"

"No," Yankowitz said. "They never saw an American blonde before, nor a girl with blue eyes, I guess. They probably think you're a phantom."

"Is that good?"

"Sure. If they like you, they'll give you the whole village."

"You seem to know a lot about these people."

"I spend a lot of time here," Yankowitz said.

"Queen of the Underworld." The Kanaka chief saluted the sacred Yankowitz' companion. "Take taro."

"I am not an underworld queen," Kathy protested angrily.

"She's a movie queen," Yankowitz corrected the chief.

Happy that his assumption had been confirmed—that Kathy was a queen—the chief invited the girl to be the guest of the village. "Village be very honored," he said. "Crazy man good friend to us. Bring powerful spirits."

"Does he mean Stump Juice?" Kathy asked.

"No. He means you."

"Okay," Kathy gaily accepted the invitation. "We'll pay you a visit."

The actress was surprised at the cleanliness of the native hut she was escorted to, and, in a short time, was gratified by the warm hospitality of the natives.

"They're nice," she remarked.

"Lousy miners," Yankowitz minimized the compliment. "They don't stand up for their rights."

"Will they let me stay here for a while?"

"Sure."

"Then I am not going back to Tontouta."

"You like being a queen?"

"No," she said. "But if I stay away from Tontouta and am found here, maybe the paratroopers won't be blamed for kidnapping me."

"You want to get these Kanakas in trouble?"

"Of course not."

"They'll get blamed for kidnapping you."

"I'll say I got lost."

"You should go back to the paratroopers."

"No," she said firmly. "I've caused them enough worry."

"They don't mind. They like to have you around."

"I need time to think. I'll stay here awhile."

"Not me," Yankowitz said. "Colonel Masterson is putting on a dance tonight at the strip. I wouldn't miss that for a vein of hard coal."

"You go," Kathy pleaded, "and don't tell Major Barrow where I am. I'll be all right."

"Okay," Yankowitz agreed. "I'll see you soon, anyway. I come up here all the time."

# 12.

When they first noticed the absence of Kathy Kennedy, the men of the First Parachute Battalion were uneasy. When many hours passed and the actress did not return and their search for her failed, they became wildly furious. A day and a half later they still had not found the girl, after a search which scoured the entire area all the way to the landing strip; then their fury turned to cold fear. Where was their beautiful Kathy Kennedy? Why had she left them? Who had taken her away?

"She was standing right here, beside this tent, talking to Private Yankowitz," the Officer of the Day recalled. "I think they went off in a jeep."

"Yankowitz!" Barrow wailed. "Of all the men in this outfit for her to hang out with. He probably took her into Nouméa for a lemonade."

"He didn't," Sergeant Fogleman stated. "The road block is still up."

"We've got to find Yankowitz before he ruins everything." Marie Belanger joined the paratroopers in their alarm. "This would have to happen just when we came up with a perfect story for Kathy to tell General Burgermeister . . ."

"And General Burgermeister has something to tell you," First Sergeant Maxwellington interrupted, speaking to Major Barrow. "He just called from Nouméa and wants to see you on the double."

"Why?"

"I don't know but he wants you to bring Private Yankowitz with you."

"Yankowitz!"

"That's right."

"It's all over," Barrow sighed. "The general must know the whole story about Miss Kennedy."

"It won't do him much good," Pfc. Howes put in. "You can't deliver her now, anyway."

"Oh, Lord!" Barrow shuddered. "If he knows we kidnapped her, and we can't produce her, he'll swear we've murdered her."

"He ought to know better than that," Corporal Martin said.

"And I don't even know where Private Yankowitz is," Barrow added.

"You'd better go to Nouméa without him, then," Captain Nugent suggested.

"That makes sense," Barrow conceded with a sneer. "I'll have to do just that."

But General Burgermeister was anxious to see Private Yankowitz.

"Where is he?" the general shouted at Major Barrow.

"I don't know, sir."

"You're hiding him."

"No, I'm not, sir," Barrow told the maddened general. "What has he done?"

Burgermeister sat back in his chair and impaled Barrow with a cruel scowl. "Do you know where Yankowitz spends the time he is supposed to be using in military training?"

"No, sir."

"In the mines," Burgermeister informed the private's commanding officer. "In the iron, chrome and nickle mines of New Caledonia."

"I can understand that, sir."

"So can I," Burgermeister agreed. "But do you have any idea what he has been doing in these mines?"

"No, sir."

"Well, Major"—Burgermeister's voice rose to an even higher pitch—"he has organized the natives who work for the French. He has drawn up a contract on behalf of the Kanakas for the operators to sign, which includes such fantastic demands as health and accident insurance coverage, portal-to-portal pay, paid holidays and profit sharing."

"He's—er—quite ambitious."

"True. And the French wish to know why they should have to recognize, and pay, for such holidays as July Fourth, Labor Day and Washington's Birthday, among other holidays which are unique with the United States."

"I don't know, but I'll have Yankowitz confined to the battalion area," Barrow promised.

"Will that get the natives back to work?"

"I don't understand."

"It's easy. The natives will not pick up a shovel until the contract is negotiated. They have delegated Yankowitz to represent them as head of their newly organized U.M.W., C.Y.O."

"You mean C.I.O.?"

"I mean the United Mine Workers, Congress of Yankowitz Organizations."

"Oh."

"The French are willing to compromise," Burgermeister said, apparently enraged at the thought of a sovereign nation having to come to terms with Private Yankowitz. "They wish to have French holidays substituted for the American days of celebration."

"I'll tell Private Yankowitz."

"That would be appreciated by the combined forces," Burgermeister said, pounding one fist into the other, trying to control his fury. "You see, the Allies need the metals, especially nickel."

"Is that all you wanted to see me about?" the greatly relieved major asked, now sure that General Burgermeister had not called him in the knowledge that Yankowitz and Kathy Kennedy were together.

"Is that all I wanted to see you about?" Burgermeister echoed in thunderous wrath. "Yes, that's all I wanted to see you about. Now you get out of here and find that maniac, Yankowitz, and have him in my office tomorrow morning or I'll have you both shipped to the Aleutians."

"Yes, sir."

"Well, get out."

"Yes, sir. But you don't have any idea where Private Yankowitz might be, do you?"

"*Get out!*"

The men of the battalion sympathized with Major Barrow but couldn't help him. Company A combed the bars and all public places in Nouméa, while Company B screened the waterfront and the Pink House. The platoons of C Company scoured all the upisland villages, shook down all hotels and, although they discovered a dozen places where they could buy wine in off-limit joints, they found no trace of the big Marine.

"Turn this island upside down," Barrow pleaded

with the men. "If we find that character, we'll probably find Miss Kennedy, too."

Thus inspired, the men resumed the search and, by evening, came to know just about every nook and cranny of New Caledonia, met more than a dozen pretty girls they never knew existed, found a forgotten champagne warehouse, came across a wonderful crap game run by the men of an Army motor transport battalion, and learned that the nurses of the Ninth Station (Army) Hospital just loved Marines. But they still didn't come up with a clue as to the whereabouts of the elusive private.

Major Barrow was almost sorry when he did discover where Yankowitz was spending his time. The formidable Colonel Masterson, formerly a corporal in C Company, visited Barrow's camp and, in no uncertain terms, told the major where his wandering private was and what it would cost Barrow and the parachutists to get him back.

Barrow glumly studied the tall, thin and scowling impersonator and shook with anger as Masterson insulted him and his command and audaciously demanded blackmail.

"What kind of an animal farm are you running, Major?" the bold phony asked.

"You ought to know," Barrow lashed back. "You're one of the prize exhibits."

Masterson generously let that impertinence go by. "I had a dance at my post the other night," the colonel-corporal told the lowly major, "and the latest addition to your side show paid us a little visit. When my orchestra declined to play a dozen polkas in a row for him, he disbanded my orchestra by reason of multiple contusions and abrasions."

"What are you talking about?"

"An interesting specimen called Yankowitz," Masterson answered. "In addition to incapacitating more than a dozen national defenders, he did considerable damage to my physical plant. I conservatively estimate that you owe me something in the nature of seven hundred dollars to replace the tents, stoves, mosquito netting, decking, rifle butts, pots, pans, and other paraphernalia he destroyed—not to mention thirteen musical instruments."

"Yankowitz!" Barrow shouted happily. "Where is he?"

"In my brig."

"Wonderful." Barrow was elated. "Let's go get him."

"You do not get him," Masterson said arrogantly, "until I get seven hundred dollars."

"Well, you won't get any seven hundred dollars from me."

"Oh, yes, I will," Masterson said with assurance. "Or you will take Yankowitz' place in my brig."

"How dare you talk to me that way, you fraud!"

"I'll expect you at five o'clock," the haughty colonel told the major. "Sharp."

"Listen, Masterson," Barrow growled, "General Burgermeister ordered me to deliver Yankowitz to him in the morning. So you better bring him over here on the double."

Colonel Masterson put his nose close to Major Barrow's. "I don't care if Franklin D. Roosevelt wants Yankowitz. He remains in my brig until you pay his bills. And if you get lippy with me, I'll lock you up for the duration of this war."

"But . . ."

"Five o'clock, sharp."

"All right."

"All right, what?"

"All right, sir."

The embarrassed major watched the presumptuous corporal stride across the area, and grimaced when Captain Nugent threw the visitor a snappy salute.

"What is this outfit coming to?" he complained to First Sergeant Maxwellington. "This is ridiculous."

"You better take it easy with Masterson," Captain Nugent cautioned the major. "He might become commandant of the whole Marine Corps some day."

Barrow ignored Nugent and fretted over his problem. "Where am I going to get seven hundred dollars to give that blackmailer? I haven't got that much money, and company funds can't match it."

"The battalion corporation might lend it to you at six percent," Corporal Crocker suggested.

"Or maybe General Burgermeister will let you borrow it." Captain Nugent tried to be helpful. "He's the only one that wants Yankowitz."

"That's a fact." Barrow frowned. "Let him and the French government bail that coal miner out."

"He might just do that," Maxwellington said seriously.

"Are you mad?"

"No. He needs Yankowitz," Maxwellington pointed out. "The whole war effort needs Yankowitz. Let the general and the French government and the mine operators pay his fine."

"Burgermeister will have a stroke if he is heisted for Yankowitz' damages," Barrow murmured. "He doesn't think he's getting a fair shake, just because Yankowitz is in this theater of war."

"Let Yankowitz write the seven hundred dollars into

one of his contracts," Maxwellington advised. "Those mine operators will never know what hit them anyway, when they begin to negotiate with our hero."

"You know," Barrow said thoughtfully, "that's not such a bad idea. I'll tell the general that Yankowitz has been captured by Masterson and that Masterson won't release him. Burgermeister will get the private out of the brig and I'll save seven hundred dollars."

"I wouldn't try to outfox Masterson if I were you," Captain Nugent warned. "He can think rings around you."

"Thank you, Captain Nugent," Barrow said bitterly. "Your loyalty touches me deeply."

"Aw, that's all right, Major."

"Can I make a suggestion?" Marie Belanger broke in.

"Sure, Marie," Barrow invited. "What is it?"

"If you don't bring back Private Yankowitz, how are you going to find out where Kathy Kennedy is?" the girl asked.

"Oh, Lord," Barrow gasped. "I never thought of that."

"Let's go over to Masterson's brig and ask Yankowitz where he hid the actress," Marie said. "After you find out where Kathy is, you can tip off General Burgermeister that Yankowitz can be picked up at the strip."

"You're going to fall on your face if you get shrewd with Masterson," Nugent said, smirking.

"You seem to be a great admirer of Corporal Masterson," Barrow snapped angrily at the captain. "How would you like me to transfer you to his command?"

"Oh, no, sir."

"Why not?"

"I'm scared to death of him."

"Well, you go requisition a jeep and a driver, and

you and I and Marie will go over to the strip and see if we can outcon your favorite con man," Barrow ordered. "This time, you may bring Masterson's mail with you."

"Yes, sir."

Corporal Crocker drove the jeep for the two officers and the French general's daughter. "If I were you," he told Major Barrow, "I'd give Masterson another seven hundred dollars if he'll guarantee to keep Yankowitz until V Day."

"If I were you," Barrow countered, "I'd keep my eyes on the road."

"It was just a thought."

"It was a good one," Barrow admitted.

Crocker drove the jeep up to the front of the brig, and Major Barrow and the others walked to the wire fence of the stockade and beckoned for Private Yankowitz to come near. Yankowitz faced the major from the inside of the brig.

"Hi, Corporal," he greeted his commanding officer.

"Hello, Yankowitz," Barrow answered.

"Did you come to get me out?"

"No. I came to find out what you have done with Kathy Kennedy."

"Well, I certainly will not tell you," Yankowitz said severely. "You ought to be ashamed of yourself."

"Why?"

"For ruining that girl's reputation, that's why," Yankowitz said crossly. "I have offered to marry her."

"Talk sense, you idiot, and tell me where she is."

"Never."

"I command you to tell me where she is."

"I won't do it."

"I'll have you arraigned for a general court-martial."

"Go ahead."

"You'll be sent to prison."

"I don't care."

"Please, Yankowitz. Tell me where the lady is."

"No."

"I'll promote you to corporal."

"Nope."

"And I'll give you a thirty-day leave."

"You can't bribe me."

"I'll have you shot."

"You're just trying to scare me."

"Why won't you tell me where the girl is?"

"Because you're a cad."

"Come on, Yankowitz," Barrow begged. "We've always been friends, and I just want to help the girl."

"She told me not to tell you where she is."

"What?"

"She says she's caused you enough trouble."

"Listen, yardbird, for the first time we've got a chance to get out of trouble, but we've got to have Kathy. Now, where is she?"

"I'll never tell."

Barrow noticed that Captain Nugent was standing at ramrod attention, and turned in irritation to find out what was the matter with his odd officer. To his dismay, he saw Masterson, the masquerader, standing behind him.

"Did you bring the seven hundred dollars, Major?" Masterson asked.

"No."

"Then why did you come over here?"

"I wanted to talk to Yankowitz."

"You'll have plenty of time. You can stay here with

him until you raise the money to cover the damages he did."

"What do you mean?"

"You can have the bunk next to his."

"Do you mean you're going to throw me in that brig, too."

"Certainly."

"Well, you will not."

"Guards," Masterson said over his shoulder, "fix bayonets and escort this major into the brig."

"Now wait a minute, Masterson," Barrow said, backing away from the brazen corporal. "You can't lock me up. I've got very important things to do."

"They'll have to wait until you pay your private's fine."

"Well, I won't pay it."

"Lock him up," Masterson commanded the guards.

"Just a moment . . ."

"You better pay him," Captain Nugent told his skipper. "He means it."

"I don't have the money."

"I'll take your note," Masterson offered generously.

"All right," Barrow said in surrender, "I'll give you an I.O.U."

"Will you endorse his note, Crocker?" Masterson asked the corporal.

"All right"—Crocker came to the aid of his commanding officer—"the corporation will back his signature."

"Fine." Masterson beamed.

"But it will cost you six percent per annum," Crocker told the badgered major.

"Very well."

Major Barrow made out the promise to pay and Corporal Crocker endorsed it, while Captain Nugent told his leader, "I told you so."

Yankowitz was deeply touched. "Gee, thanks, Corporal," he said to Major Barrow. "I didn't know you liked me so much."

"I don't like you at all," Barrow hissed. "I'm merely buying my way out of this horrible situation."

"Don't you want Private Yankowitz?" Masterson asked.

"No, I do not. You can keep him forever."

"If he stays here," Masterson threatened, "it will cost you ten dollars a day for his subsistence and quarters."

"I'll give you ten dollars if you'll hold him overnight," Barrow told Masterson. "I've got to deliver him to General Burgermeister in the morning, so the mine operators can negotiate a contract with him. I don't want him in my area and I can't take a chance on losing him again. Captain Nugent will pick him up at 0800."

"That will be ten dollars in advance." Masterson held out his hand.

Back in his jeep, Barrow moaned, "We should never have come over here."

"You should have listened to me," Captain Nugent said smugly.

"It was a mistake," Barrow mumbled.

"A pretty expensive one," Crocker agreed.

"And we have nothing to show for our trouble or your money," Marie added. "We still don't know where Kathy is."

"And we never will if we wait for Yankowitz to tell us," Barrow sighed.

"If he had a brain," Crocker observed, "we could out-think him."

"We're going to have to outthink him anyway," Marie said. "Sooner or later that general is going to trace Kathy to the First Parachute Battalion."

"All right," Barrow challenged, "where would Yankowitz have taken her?"

"Where does Yankowitz spend his time?" Marie asked.

"Either in the brig or in the mines," Barrow answered.

"It's unlikely that he would have hidden her in a brig," Marie pointed out.

"But it's not unlikely that he would have hidden her in a mine," Barrow said excitedly.

"And if he's organized all the mine workers on this island," Marie said, "he must be spending a lot of time in the mines."

"And the mine workers are his friends," Crocker put in.

"Well"—Captain Nugent got things going—"where are the mines?"

"All over the island," Marie said, dropping a damper on the enthusiasm of the men.

"Oh."

"But the busiest ones are in the Chaine Centrale east of Bourail," Marie continued.

"Okay," Barrow said loudly, "let's start there."

The jeep did not turn into the camp of the paratroopers but crossed the bridge over the Dumbea River and continued upisland. At Bourail, they turned off into the interisland highway and sped toward the interior and the rich mines.

"We'll pace off every inch of the mine shafts," Barrow said. "We'll probably find her in one of them."

"Oh, no, you won't," Marie corrected. "There isn't any shaft mining in New Caledonia. These are pit mines."

"Good." Barrow changed course. "There must be mine buildings, and Yankowitz left her in one of them."

"Maybe."

While the confused Kanakas looked on, Major Barrow ran from the tool shed to the small engine room, peeking behind the machinery, circling the buildings and searching behind the rocks and trees nearby. He finally stopped in exhaustion.

"That fella almost as crazy as the giant," one Kanaka whispered to another.

"Yeah," the second Kanaka agreed. "Those American Marines are all crazy."

Captain Nugent wasn't much help during the search. He glanced uneasily at the ugly Kanakas, and each time one approached him, he shied away and either ran over to Marie Belanger and Corporal Crocker or hid behind Major Barrow.

"That fella is as dizzy as Yankowitz," one of the Kanakas said in admiration.

"Well"—the other was more conservative—"pretty near."

"Those two fellas must be high-ranking spirits," they agreed. "Plenty sacred to be so unbalanced."

"And we're plenty lucky," they congratulated themselves. "Pretty soon we'll have a collection of all the lunatics on the island."

"We are the favored of the gods."

Major Barrow was examining the Kanakas from a distance. He was appalled by their size, thick shoulders, massive chests, bulging arms and wicked-looking knives. He was especially impressed by their brilliant orange hair.

"Are the natives friendly?" he whispered to Marie.

"They're as harmless as babies," Marie assured him.

"They look ferocious."

"They're not."

"Why don't you ask them if they've seen Miss Kennedy?" Captain Nugent asked Barrow.

"That's a good idea," Barrow answered. "You go ask them."

"I don't want to," Nugent said, looking askance at the natives. "You ask them."

"I don't think I will," Barrow hedged. "I don't like the way they swing those knives."

"I'll ask them," Marie volunteered. "They're very gentle."

"Go ahead, Marie," Corporal Crocker encouraged her. "We're right behind you."

"You fellas seen American girl with white hair?" Marie asked, walking up to the Kanaka leader. "Eyes like water, skin like clouds."

"You betcha."

"Where is she?"

"In village."

The three Marines and the French girl were elated.

"Bring her here," Marie ordered the Kanaka.

"Never happen."

"Why not?"

"She our new queen. Very sacred. Personal friend of most crazy Yankowitz."

"This fella with gold leaves on shoulder number one boss of Yankowitz," Marie told the native.

"Impossible," the Kanaka contradicted. "He's not half as crazy as the giant."

"He is much crazier," Marie argued.

"I am not," Barrow said in fury.

"Yes, you are," Marie told him. "You had better be if you want to get Kathy."

"Why?"

"To these people," the girl explained, "lunatics are sacred."

"There must be an easier way," Barrow protested.

"Nothing comes easy for the First Parachute Battalion," Crocker philosophized.

"Will you take us to the queen?" Marie asked the native.

"Glad to. Very proud of queen. One powerful spirit."

"She sure is," Barrow agreed. "She carries the power of life and death over us."

"I believe it," the Kanaka said.

To the dismay of the major, before the Kanaka chief would let him visit the movie queen, the native men, with their long machetes, were mustered and placed, as a cordon, around Kathy's building. Apparently the chief meant it when he said that the actress was going to remain as the guest of the village.

"Kathy, are you all right?" Barrow asked with great concern when he was ushered into her presence.

"Sure," she answered. "I am hiding out here until the pressure is off the parachutists, and then I'll give myself up. I'll tell the general I escaped from the jeep driver and got lost."

"He won't believe you," Barrow said dejectedly. "One of these days his recreation officer is going to come across Corporal Martin's picture and then he'll lower the boom."

"I'll give myself up right away, then," the girl valiantly offered. "I'll get to Nouméa before they find Martin's picture."

"We've got a better idea," Marie said. "We've got a story for you to tell that will not only get everyone out of trouble, but will make you and the parachutists great heroes."

"Honest?"

"Sure." Marie told the actress of the wonderful plot she and the paratroopers had worked out. "You'll be the greatest female war heroine since Joan of Arc."

Kathy thought over the imaginative production Marie had outlined. "I'll do it," she squealed in delight. "They'll have to film the story of my life in two parts."

"Well, let's go," Barrow enthused.

"I've got to thank these wonderful natives before I go anywhere," Kathy told the major. "They couldn't have been nicer to me."

"Of course."

But although the Kanakas expressed nothing but affection for their queen and friendliness toward the new visitors, they formed an ominous circle around the Americans and the French girl and declined to let Kathy Kennedy leave their village. Kathy, more than welcome, had been left by the number one madman, and the natives would be remiss if they allowed the golden goddess to depart before they received an okay from the boss lunatic.

"Crazy man say goddess stay here," the chief apologized.

"But I am Yankowitz' commanding officer," Barrow explained to the chief. "Yankowitz does what I say."

"You wish," Corporal Crocker muttered.

"You are quite crazy," the Kanaka admitted, "but the giant is crazier than you."

"That's not what I'm talking about," Barrow said patiently. "I am Yankowitz' boss."

"Compared to you"—the Kanaka held his ground— "Yankowitz is howling mad."

"Thank you," the frustrated major gratefully acknowledged the compliment, "but we are still talking about two different things."

"You'll have to convince the chief that you are crazier than Yankowitz," Marie informed the major. "You've got to overrule the private."

"I haven't been able to yet," Barrow said grimly. "I haven't been able to overrule anyone since I've been in the Pacific."

"I wonder how Yankowitz convinced the natives that he was so crazy," Marie said.

"It was easy for him, I guess," Barrow replied. "All he had to do was act natural."

"Go ahead"—Captain Nugent encouraged Major Barrow—"act natural."

"Will you leave me alone?" Barrow shouted at the captain. "All you ever do is add to my problems."

"What's so hard about acting natural?" Nugent wanted to know.

"I am acting natural," Barrow snarled. "I always act natural."

"You are considerably unbalanced," the Kanaka chief

told Barrow in admiration after watching him explode at the captain. "How long have you been crazy?"

"Only for the past few minutes," Barrow shouted in anger.

"You're improving," the Kanaka admitted.

"You don't seem much different to me," Nugent consoled the furious major.

"Will you all shut up?" Barrow yelled.

"You're doing fine," Marie told the major. "The natives are bringing you gifts of fruits and vegetables."

"I don't want their fruits and vegetables," Barrow groaned.

"They gave me a whole plantation," Kathy said modestly.

"I guess I'm safe," Nugent said gratefully. "They haven't even offered me a banana."

"If you people persist," the frantic major wailed, looking at the ring of machetes in the hands of the Kanakas, "I'll crack up. I've never been so close to the lockup ward before."

"Bring this man more taro," the delighted chief ordered his tribesmen.

"Keep your stupid taro," Barrow screamed at the Kanaka. "You're not going to convince me that I'm crazy."

"You've convinced me," the chief said, beaming.

"All right, then," Barrow shouted, "release the queen to me."

"Sorry," the chief hedged. "You aren't that crazy—and neither are we."

"But, Chief"—Kathy joined the major—"I've got to leave. I've got to jump from a plane."

"Wow!" the chief and his followers marveled. "I'd like to see that."

"Please, Chief," Marie chimed in, "let her go. She's got to go back to her own country."

"To the underworld?" the chief asked eagerly.

"Certainly not!" Kathy bristled. "I'm going back to Hollywood."

"With Yankowitz?"

"No."

"This is hopeless." Marie voiced the panic and disappointment of her group. "They'll never let her go until Yankowitz says it's all right."

"But we've got to get her out of here today," Barrow said. "Our time is running out."

Marie made one more strong effort to solve the problem. "Please let my sister go with these men," she pleaded with the chief.

"She's your sister?"

"Yes. And Yankowitz will be angry if you keep her any longer."

"We don't want Yankowitz angry with us," the chief said uneasily.

"He will come here and put the evil eye on your village, and all the houses will fall and the crops will die," Marie threatened.

"And he can do it," Captain Nugent added.

The Kanakas weren't sure. "What if this is a trick?" they asked each other. "Yankowitz will turn us into fish."

"I'll stay and take the queen's place until Yankowitz comes," Marie offered.

"You friend of Yankowitz?" the chief demanded.

"Sure."

"Marie," Barrow interrupted, "what are you saying?"

"We've got to get her out of here," Marie answered.

"I'll stay as hostage until Yankowitz tells his friends that everything is all right."

"Well, I won't let you do it. They might hurt you," Barrow said. "And who knows what Yankowitz might tell them?"

"We'll have to take that chance," Marie said with authority. "You take Kathy with you, and tomorrow get Yankowitz out of the brig and bring him out here so I can be freed."

"I'd give that some thought," Captain Nugent cautioned. "That Yankowitz does more disappearing tricks than a Hindu."

"We've got to take that chance," Marie said unequivocally.

"It's awfully nice of you to offer . . ." Barrow began.

"Is it all right with you, Chief?" Marie interrupted. "You'll take the queen's place until Yankowitz come here?"

"Yes."

"All right."

As Captain Nugent, Corporal Crocker and Kathy Kennedy got into the jeep, Major Barrow took Marie aside.

"I appreciate what you're doing," he began.

She waited for him to proceed.

"It seems that you are always helping me out of some kind of unpleasant situation."

She smiled but remained silent.

"Marie, I want you to know how much you have come to mean to me, well, all of us," he blurted in a rush of words. "I mean, I . . ."

"Yes?" she encouraged him.

"Hey, what do you say, Major?" Corporal Crocker

interrupted with a shout. "Are you in this theater of war for business or pleasure?"

"He's talking business," Nugent reprimanded Crocker.

"I know," Crocker agreed. "Let's get on with the pleasure."

"I'll be here to get you tomorrow," Barrow told the brave French girl. "Don't worry."

"I won't." She sighed happily as he left. "I won't worry at all.

# 13.

With its horn blaring for attention, Barrow's jeep careened into the camp. The major leaped from the vehicle and commanded the men who were running up to greet the actress, to pass the word for assembly. In a few seconds men were converging on him from every section of the base. They were delighted to welcome back their lovely actress but were sobered by the serious look on the major's face.

"Is everything all set to get Miss Kennedy out of here?" he asked First Sergeant Maxwellington.

"Yes, sir."

"Fogleman," Barrow called, "are you sure Kathy can make a jump and tumble without killing herself."

"Yes, sir, but . . ."

"But what?"

"We've only had that sweet, adorable, lovely doll with us for a few days," Fogleman said. "Can't we wait until next month?"

"No."

The whole battalion glanced sadly at their dream and then scowled at their commanding officer.

"Wars aren't won in a day," Fogleman persisted.

"But they're lost in a day," Barrow countered, "and it might be any minute for us."

"Yes, sir."

"Martin, Crocker and Maxwellington," Barrow ordered. "You men take Miss Kennedy into my tent and go over the whole plan again with her."

"Yes, sir."

"Checkoway," Barrow continued, "you sneak through the woods to the Tontouta strip and see what kind of planes are available."

"I already did, sir," Checkoway responded. "The only thing over there is a C-47."

"What's wrong with that?"

"It's a transport. We could put a whole company in it."

"Okay," Major Barrow said expansively, "we'll put a company in it."

"Can you fly the thing, Checkoway?" Howes wanted to know.

"I don't know," Checkoway answered. "I learn as I go."

"I think I'll go answer the phone," Captain Nugent said.

"You stay right here," Barrow commanded. "You're going to act as jump master."

"I wish the boys in the office could see me now," Nugent whined. "Back in the office."

"Saddle up," the major said dramatically. "We've got to chance it. Take some kind of a cable so we can rig up for the static lines. We've got to land together."

The men prepared for the flight and jump while Major Barrow went to officers' country to alert the movie actress.

"Have you got your story down pat?" he asked Kathy.

"Perfect."

"Do you still want to go through with this?"

"Yes," she said. "But I'll miss you and the men."

"We'll all miss you, Kathy."

B Company advanced into the woods ahead of the jumping party, clearing a path with machetes; the actress and the major and the company followed.

"Everybody got plenty of ammunition?" Sergeant Fogleman asked the troopers.

"Yes."

"Does Martin know where to park the truck?" Barrow asked.

"Yes, sir."

"Don't forget to stash those chutes as soon as we land."

"Right, sir."

Crocker reported to the commanding officer. He had been watching the pilots through the window of their shack.

"They found the stack of comic books I planted in the shack," he said. "They wouldn't know it if the roof fell in on them."

"Curtain, everybody," Kathy giggled.

"I think she means 'curtains,'" Private Lincoln said.

"Well, don't stand there like sailors," Checkoway commanded. "Get in the plane."

After an agonizingly slow start, Checkoway managed to get the giant plane off the ground, removing the tin smokestack from the pilot's shack as he zoomed over the building. A few minutes later, Captain Nugent gave the first of the three commands. "Coming on the range."

The men stood up, checked each other's parachutes, and snapped their static lines to the cable.

A few seconds later Nugent shouted, "Stand by."

The men and the movie queen hurriedly rechecked their gear.

"Go!"

Heroically charging toward the entrance of the plane, leading his men in the daring maneuver, Major Barrow stopped suddenly, his face blanching and his knees trembling.

"I just remembered something," he gasped.

"What?" Kathy, behind him, asked.

"I forgot to take tumbling lessons."

"It's too late now," Captain Nugent announced as the men behind the major began to pile up in a congested line. "You'll have to leave this plane."

"It's all right," Barrow sought to excuse himself. "I'll wait here."

"If you don't get out of that doorway," Sergeant Fogleman shouted, "we'll be in the middle of the Pacific before we jump."

"Go ahead, boys," Barrow offered generously. "Don't worry about me. I'll be all right—right here."

"Get out of the way," the men were now shouting in chorus. "You're holding up the war."

"Go ahead, Major," Kathy encouraged him. "You can do it."

He looked out into the void, his eyes wide with terror, and grasped the doorway to steady himself.

"I'm afraid of height," he cried.

"Get out," the man bellowed.

"Don't go away mad, Major, just go away."

"I can't even stand to ride in an elevator," Barrow wailed.

"Push him out, someone."

"I wish I were in the submarine service."

"So do we. Get out!"

"Major," Kathy said, pushing him and trying to free his hands from their frozen grip on the sides of the door, "please step outside."

"I don't want to. I couldn't bear to step outside."

"It's all right. There's nothing there."

"That's what I mean."

"He'll make us jump right down the smokestack of the nickel smelter," Crocker complained. "Why doesn't he think of someone besides himself?"

"Control yourself, Major," Captain Nugent pleaded. "Get down to earth."

"Don't you get funny with me, Nugent," the pale major breathed. "I don't feel well."

"The fresh air will do you good," Kathy suggested.

"It's killing me."

"You're going to kill us all."

"Tell Checkoway to keep on going," Lincoln called. "We might as well fly her all the way to San Francisco, now."

"This exercise is dismissed," Barrow whined. "Fall out."

"We'll fall out if you'll stop blocking the door," the men snarled.

There was only one thing to do. Kathy braced herself against the man behind her and gave Barrow a boot in his majority. He spun into space, and the rest followed him.

"Take me back," Barrow shrieked into the prop wash.

"Walk," suggested Sergeant Fogleman, swinging in his harness beside the major.

"I can't tumble, Fogleman."

"You'll be all right," Fogleman said. "The air is nice and heavy."

"It is?"

"Sure. Can't you tell?"

"No."

"You're going to be all right," the expert assured him.

"I hope so."

Fogleman was right. The few bumps he got did not decommission the major.

The plane was circling back to Tontouta when the men and the girl hit the ground. Swiftly the jumping party sought out Martin's truck and tossed their parachutes into it.

"Take off, Martin," the driver was ordered.

"Yes, sir."

As the truck roared away, the parachutists began to blaze away at the nearby water's edge with rifles, Johnson light machine guns and Browning automatic rifles. The sound of gunfire could be heard well beyond Nouméa, where one detachment of Marines rushed to surround the nickel smelter to protect it from saboteurs, and the regiments were broken out on a dead run toward the beaches to repulse an enemy landing party. Ships in the harbor were ordered to head for the open sea; the giant triangle in Place des Cocotiers sounded alarm, and volunteers of the civilian defense organization manned their posts. Calls were put through to the surrounding towns that Nouméa was closed off and all traffic was routed back into the island. The city engineer was ordered to black out the town, and threw the main switch. Hotel patrons, bar customers and officers in military posts were thrown into panic as their lights went out and power failed.

A Chinese laundryman, on his way home from his shop, was fired upon by French troops, who mistook him for a Japanese and sorely wounded him in the leg. The laundryman's screams and the sound of gunfire were interpreted as a running street battle, and windows were boarded up and barricades erected in the intersections of the main roads. Several people, carrying both Japanese and American flags, appeared on the streets to assure the victors that they were friendly to either side. Guards in the city prison panicked when gunfire was heard under the prison window, and the entire prison colony of New Caledonia rushed into the streets, to the terror of the people.

Kathy, putting on an Academy Award performance, tore her clothes, rolled in the soft dirt and mussed up her pretty hair. She lay sobbing at the feet of the paratroopers when the white-faced General Burgermeister, with an armed guard, drove up in his jeep.

"Miss Kennedy," he shouted in elation, yet with concern, "are you all right?"

"Yes," she cried. "They came just in time. They saved me. It was horrible."

"Who saved you?"

She pointed to the paratroopers, who stood holding their still-smoking weapons.

"From whom, Miss Kennedy?"

"From them." She pointed toward the sea and shuddered.

"What's going on here, Major Barrow?" the general asked, dubious, worried, suspicious.

"We've been combing this island for days, looking for Miss Kennedy, General," Major Barrow said to his superior with a strong tone of anger in his voice. "If no one else could find the lady, we believed we could. And we had to if we wanted to get one look at her after that stinking bulletin you sent us."

Senator Patterson joined the group. "The general will send you a written apology in the morning," the politician promised the parachutists, giving Burgermeister a withering glance. "And the paratroopers will receive the thanks and congratulations of Congress."

"I'll be glad to send you and your men an apology," Burgermeister told Barrow sincerely. "And my own thanks and congratulations."

"Thank you, sir."

Burgermeister turned to Miss Kennedy. "Come, my dear. We'll get you straightened out and you can tell Naval Intelligence what happened."

After Crocker drove Major Barrow and the captain safely back to the camp in the recon truck he "borrowed" in Nouméa, the major asked for Checkoway. He was in the mess tent, drinking coffee and studying a handbook on airplanes.

"You landed okay?" the major asked, relieved.

"Pancaked. Couldn't find the controls for the landing gear."

"But you got away from the strip all right."

"Easy. Some of the boys from A Company showed up in M.P. gear and arrested me. They brought me back here."

"At Tontouta they fell for that old gag?"

"Didn't you know?" Checkoway quizzed the major.

"Colonel Masterson, the commanding officer over there, is one of our corporals from C Company."

"So I heard," Major Barrow admitted.

The men gathered around the radio, waiting for the first short-wave broadcast from the States. It was wonderful.

"Captured by the last gang of Vichy French on the island," the commentator reported excitedly, "Miss Kennedy was held prisoner for ten horror-filled days. On the eve of her execution, demanded by the Nazis because she refused to give information concerning ship movements and troop stations, the gang was attacked and routed by the fearless men of the First Parachute Battalion, who drove them into the sea. Miss Kennedy said that the paratroopers killed and wounded several of the Vichyites, but that they were dragged into their escape boat by their colleagues. The boat has not been found and the entire gang is believed to have been drowned. Miss Kennedy couldn't give much information on the questions put to her, since her captors spoke no English and she speaks no French."

Barrow was elated when Kathy Kennedy told the world, in glowing terms, of his gallantry and bravery. According to her statements, embroidered by her press agent, Barrow was the most outstanding soldier since the Duke of Wellington. Telegrams from the swivel-chair commandos back in the paymaster's department were a source of pleasure and pride to him. The Pentagon warriors and the midnight marauders from the Mayfair Bar now had their own hero—Good Old Major Barrow. And a congratulatory message from the commandant of the Corps implied that the boys back in Washington, at all levels, had finally taken notice of the brilliant commanding officer of the First Parachute Battalion.

Hollywood and Broadway were also elated, it seemed, and her studio awarded Miss Kennedy the biggest contract in its history. The White House sent words of praise to General Burgermeister and a Presidential Unit Citation to the First Parachute Battalion. Kathy sent the troopers a wire expressing her wish that they could be with her on her ticker-tape parade down Broadway.

"It ain't going to be the same around here without that girl." Whoever said that, spoke for the entire battalion.

# 14.

Early the next morning, Major Barrow, accompanied by Captain Nugent and two men sworn in as guards, arrived at the brig at Tontouta strip to get Private Yankowitz. The major was anxious to rescue the pretty hostage he had left in the Kanaka village.

"Aren't you taking this man to Nouméa?" Masterson asked as he nodded for the guards to release the private.

"No. I've got to take him some place more important."

"I understand that the general has assembled the island's outstanding industrialists and some persons of political weight in his office who wish to have a session with your pet baboon," Masterson pointed out. "The general might develop a complex if you persist in treating him this way."

"There's nothing I can do about it," Barrow said lamely. "I've got to take Yankowitz some place else."

"Sure," Masterson said. "But just for the record, what could be more important to a Marine major than a Marine general?"

"A woman," Captain Nugent answered brightly.

"That makes sense," Masterson conceded.

"Thank you," Barrow said, moving hurriedly toward his jeep.

"But why would you want to take Yankowitz on a

date?" Masterson continued to annoy Major Barrow. "If she has a friend, I'd be glad to go along."

"You don't understand," Barrow stated.

"I confess, I don't," Masterson agreed. "And I doubt that General Burgermeister will, either."

"I'll see General Burgermeister later," Barrow said as he got into his jeep.

"Fine. I'll tell him," Masterson promised. "He'll appreciate your thoughtfulness."

"Just tell him I have something very important to take care of."

"I will. As long as it's more important than the war, I'm sure he'll understand."

On the trip to the pit mines, Barrow explained the situation to Private Yankowitz. "I had to leave Marie in Miss Kennedy's place," he said. "The natives won't let her go until you say it's okay."

"I wonder why."

"So do I."

"They think you're a great authority because you're crazy," Captain Nugent assured Private Yankowitz.

"Is that so?"

"We tried to convince them that Major Barrow is crazier than you."

"How did you make out?"

"We failed," Barrow interrupted. "Happily, we failed."

"You want to try again?"

"No."

"Where's Kathy?" Yankowitz asked.

"She has left us," Barrow answered. "She's in Nouméa and will be returning to the States very soon."

"She shouldn't travel alone in her condition," the coal miner said.

"There's nothing wrong with her condition."

"If I was in the village yesterday, neither of you would have left until you married the girl," Yankowitz stated bluntly.

"That's all I would have needed," Barrow said. "You cost me seven hundred dollars the other day. You might as well take my freedom."

"I'll owe you the seven hundred dollars," the private offered generously.

"First Sergeant Maxwellington said it will be all right to write the seven hundred dollars into the contract you're going to negotiate with the mine operators," Captain Nugent told Private Yankowitz. "If it wasn't for them, the major could have let you stay in the brig until Masterson threw you out."

"Okay," Yankowitz promised irresponsibly. "I'll take care of the matter."

"This I've got to see," Barrow said.

Marie greeted the Marines cheerfully and assured Major Barrow that she had been well treated by the Kanakas.

"I almost hate to leave," she reported.

"Regardless," Barrow interrupted, "that doesn't minimize the deep feeling of gratitude I feel toward you for your help."

"I was glad to do it," Marie said simply.

"You'll also be glad to know your little idea went off like clockwork," Captain Nugent informed her. "We not only got rid of Kathy Kennedy but our unit is to be decorated for saving her from the enemy."

And the Kanakas were happy that their hero, Yankowitz, was not displeased because they had released the blonde goddess. And since they were accompanied by the natives' favorite madman, the Marines were made more than welcome and a feast was arranged in their honor.

"Yankowitz will get us all a raise in pay," the Kanakas rejoiced.

"And paid holidays," Barrow said.

"And your seven hundred dollars," Nugent added.

"But tell them we'll come back for the feast some other day," Barrow instructed Yankowitz. "We're already hours late for our meeting with General Burgermeister."

"He'll have to wait," Yankowitz said firmly. "My friends come first."

"We can't keep the general and all those mine operators waiting while we have a party," Barrow tried to explain. "Burgermeister will murder us both."

"He'll wait if he wants these mines back in production," the big private told the major.

"Yankowitz," Barrow said, losing patience, "I order you to tell these people that the feast is off."

"That would not be polite."

"I don't care if it's polite or not." Barrow was losing his temper as well as his patience. "You've cost me nothing but trouble since you came out here, and, because of you, I'm going to be scalped when I get back to Nouméa. Now get in the jeep."

"You don't know anything about negotiating a contract," Yankowitz haughtily told his commanding officer. "You've got to make those people wait."

"You're in the Marine Corps now, you idiot," Barrow

shouted. "Privates do not make generals wait for anything."

"Then it's about time someone told those generals the facts of life," Yankowitz argued. "We're fighting for democracy, ain't we?"

"Shut up and let's get going."

The Kanakas, anxious to please the sacred private, formed their ring of steel around the major and the other Marines. If Yankowitz said the Marines were to stay, they would stay.

"Yankowitz," Marie pleaded, "he's only trying to help you. All the operators are assembled and waiting in Nouméa so that they can give the Kanakas the benefits you worked for in their behalf. If you don't go to town now, the general will transfer you to Guadalcanal and the contracts won't be negotiated."

"He wouldn't dare."

"Oh, yes, he would."

"Would he, Corporal?"

"Of course."

Yankowitz wavered. "I guess maybe we'd better go to Nouméa. I don't trust that general."

"I think you're right."

"We'll be back," Yankowitz told the Kanakas as he followed Barrow to the jeep.

"Just like MacArthur," Captain Nugent added.

The mine operators shared General Burgermeister's wrath, and they looked up in glum fury when Major Barrow escorted Private Yankowitz into the general's office.

"Nice of you to drop in, Major," Burgermeister

growled. "We expected you at 0900 and it is now 1430."

"I would have been here sooner, sir," Barrow alibied, "but I had to take Yankowitz away on an important matter."

"I expected all along that you and your wonder-boy were in collusion," Burgermeister growled. "Have you completed your conspiracy?"

"I have nothing to do with Yankowitz' escapades," Major Barrow assured the general. "I am angry with him for meddling in things that do not concern him and I apologize for keeping you and these other gentlemen waiting so long."

"That's all right," the spokesman for the mine operators told the major. "We don't have a thing in the world to do until Yankowitz permits us to reopen the mines. There's nothing we *can* do."

"Well, Corporals"—Yankowitz' voice filled the room —"let us proceed to remove the shackles from the honest laborers of New Caledonia."

The spokesman bristled. "Are you implying that we are oppressing our workers?"

"No, Corporal," Yankowitz answered. "It's just that you've practically made slaves of them."

"The international crisis compels us to take your outrageous demands seriously," the mine operator said, "and we are willing to sign your preposterous contract, with certain amendments."

"What amendments?" Yankowitz wanted to know.

"We wish to substitute Bastille Day for July Fourth, and we would prefer to recognize either Lafayette or Napoleon in place of George Washington."

"What's the matter with you people?" Yankowitz was shocked. "Ain't you patriotic?"

"Yes, we are patriotic, but we did not have the good fortune to be born Americans. Try to understand that by accident of birth, we happen to be Frenchmen and adore the institutions of France."

"That's no excuse," Yankowitz reprimanded the Frenchmen. "Don't you know there's a war on?"

"We don't follow you."

"You should select patriots and patriotic occasions to celebrate," Yankowitz patiently pointed out.

"The days we suggest have wide patriotic implications," one of the men explained to Yankowitz. "Lafayette and Napoleon were to France what Washington was to the United States."

"That's the truth." Major Barrow tried to reason with his private. "They were great French leaders."

"If you say so, Corporal," Yankowitz said dubiously. "But what is this Bastille?"

"The Bastille was a prison in France . . ." another mine operator began.

"Just what I thought," Yankowitz mocked. "A little reminder to the workers that you'll imprison them if they stand up for their rights."

"You're all mixed up, Yankowitz," General Burgermeister roared. "The workers were liberated from the Bastille by the patriots."

"Who put the workers in prison?" Yankowitz asked.

"The government."

"See!" Yankowitz exclaimed. "Turning criminals loose to plunder the working men and women."

"We're getting nowhere," the operators whined in unison to the general. "This man is deliberately holding up the production of our mines."

"Please, Yankowitz," Major Barrow implored. "These

men know more about their institutions than you do, and they have carefully considered the most appropriate holidays. Sign the contract so your friends can get back to work."

"What about back pay?" Yankowitz remained stubborn.

"That is all worked out."

"All right," Yankowitz said, making a concession to his commanding officer. "After you pay Corporal Barrow seven hundred dollars, I'll sign."

"Why should we pay Major Barrow seven hundred dollars?" the spokesman screamed. "He's taking advantage of us. It's a shake-down."

"Legal fees," Yankowitz stated authoritatively.

"Legal fees for what?"

"Legal fees for getting me out of the brig so that I could come down here today," Yankowitz said.

"Barrow," General Burgermeister thundered, "you're a pirate. You're putting the Chinese shoe on these men."

"Well, I did incur an expense of seven hundred dollars," Barrow told the general.

"You have no business taking outside employment," the general raged. "Your time belongs to the government."

"I was on government time," Barrow said limply.

"That's what I mean," Burgermeister shouted. "You're playing both ends against the middle."

"Well, I don't sign until the corporal is reimbursed," Yankowitz said firmly.

"All right," the spokesman said, defeated, "we'll pay the seven hundred dollars and raise the price of ore to the United States."

"You will not," Yankowitz said blandly. "You ain't going to take advantage of us."

"We'll absorb the loss," the industrialist said in surrender, shooting General Burgermeister a look of unutterable disgust. "As this private seems to have backed New Caledonia's industries and his own branch of the service into a corner, we have no choice but to go along."

"Sign that document and get out," Burgermeister commanded Yankowitz, "and take your unscrupulous major with you."

"Don't you talk to Corporal Barrow that way," Yankowitz threatened, "or the mines will close forever."

"Get out."

"We're going, sir," Barrow said in horror as he dragged the private toward the door. "Don't listen to this man. He's crazy."

"I wish we were only half as crazy," one of the mine owners said bitterly as Barrow and his private left. "It just doesn't pay to be sane any more."

# 15.

In his tent, some days later, Major Barrow reviewed the events of the past few weeks and shook his head in disbelief that so much could have happened in such a short time. There was one consolation. He and the men had forgotten their feud while they coped with the terrible emergency the kidnapping of the movie actress had created. Absorbed in the problem of getting Kathy Kennedy out of his camp, the major had been only vaguely aware of and only vaguely concerned with the reappearance of the insolent signs over the doors of the men's tents and the Parisian pin-up pictures in their foot lockers. Under their bunks, the major knew, the men had again laid in enough supplies to stock a hospital and a variety store. But it didn't seem so important now. He felt that he had just emerged from a battle of life and death, and the small stockpile of material goods did not seem so significant as it had a short while ago. He was aware that out in the company areas a first sergeant was giving the prisoners-at-large a series of lectures on how to beat a court-martial, and that lessons in Japanese were being held in the afternoons. In the tent of the armorer, Corporal Martin and his cronies were cutting up sheets and mattress covers and converting them into genuine Japanese battle flags. In the river, the guards were frolicking while the men doing brig time were holding submachine guns. New and ribald verses to the "Marine's Hymn" were being written by the Board of Directors of the corporation as they enjoyed their daily cocktail hour. And the officers were still flipping coins to see who would draw the duty as Officer of the Day. He couldn't seem to remember when the last reveille had been held.

"Well," he sighed, thinking back to the visit of Kathy Kennedy and Yankowitz' presumptuous fling into unionism, "I'm glad it's all behind me. The men will settle down now and I'll run a quiet camp. We'll just keep out of General Burgermeister's way and all will be smooth sailing."

Sitting on the edge of his bunk, Major Barrow cut another hole in his belt so that his trousers would not fall down when he walked through his area of command. He smiled happily as he counted the several other new holes in his belt.

"Nine inches," he estimated. "I must have lost forty pounds chasing those paratroopers up and down the hills."

He smiled, pleased with himself, as though he had deliberately set out to get himself back into shape—and succeeded.

"Of course," he added in his thoughts, "I have picked up a few gray hairs. Well, they'll do until the campaign bars come along."

And a very nice thing now happened to Major Barrow. As he mused contentedly in his quarters, Corporal Martin and Pfc. Howes knocked at his door and asked permission to enter.

"Come in, men," Barrow invited.

Martin saluted respectfully and handed the major a

note. Barrow read it, his chest swelling and his eyes dampening:

> *The men of C Company cordially invite you to take Stump Juice with them at two. R.S.V.P.*

"My compliments to the men of C Company," Barrow formally responded, "and tell them that I am pleased to accept their invitation."

General Burgermeister also had occasion to review the past few weeks, but his conclusions were not as gratifying as Major Barrow's. Burning from embarrassment after having had to join the New Caledonian industrialists in surrendering to that insolent paratrooper private and still confused and angry over the kidnapping of the actress and her unconvincing rescue, he fumed in frustration and ineffectual fury.

"Some day," he ranted to his aide, Colonel Ward, "I'm going to make that ghoul Barrow wish he was in Tokyo."

"We might all be in Tokyo sooner than you realize it, sir," the colonel said, handing Burgermeister a dispatch that had just come in from Washington via Honolulu. "You're to execute the initial actions for the up-coming big push."

Burgermeister hurriedly glanced at the communiqué. "You know," he said, an evil grin spreading over his face, "I think I know how we can clip the wings of two birds with one invasion. Get me a jeep."

"Here comes the pocket battleship," Captain Nugent informed Major Barrow, as the general got out of his jeep and strode across the area toward them. "Stand by for a broadside."

"You men think you're pretty smart," the general said, running his eyes over the paratroopers and their commander.

"Yes, sir."

"Well, so do I." Burgermeister smiled expansively. "Very smart."

The men exchanged nods of agreement.

"Now, about that trip back to the States," Burgermeister began.

The faces of the men lit up.

"It's out," the general went on.

"He's a fugitive from Honshu," Sergeant Fogleman observed.

"I'm trying to remember why I hated Japs," Corporal Martin said. "They must have done something awful to top that beast."

"I almost had you," Burgermeister told the major and his men. "If the eyesight of my recreation officer hadn't given out on him, I still think he would have identified a gang of scoundrels that would have made any Vichy outfit look like a convention of Sunday-school teachers— namely, the First Parachute Battalion."

"General," Barrow said seriously, "you know that my men wouldn't have done anything like kidnapping that girl."

"I know," Burgermeister answered, still smiling but not able to repress the snarl in his voice. "You and the troopers are all going to hell without a sin."

"Why," Barrow pointed out, "we rescued her from death."

"Yes," the general said sarcastically, "and you should be rewarded."

The men looked uneasily at each other.

"His idea of a reward," Private Lincoln speculated, "would be a firing squad with dum-dum bullets."

"Or a compulsory re-enlistment," Crocker said.

"So I'm going to let you men take a little trip," Burgermeister said gaily. "Pack up and get ready to move out."

"Where are we going?" Barrow asked hopefully. "New Zealand? Australia?"

"No," Burgermeister boomed, his laughter offending the parachutists. "There's a push coming up in a few days and you're going to be the first to hit the beach."

"He did it again," Howes complained to Martin. "He's taking advantage of his rank."

"Yeah," Martin said sadly. "All he thinks of is war."

Major Barrow was convinced that the general was having the last laugh. The tough old leader had succeeded in turning the tables on him so effectively that Barrow's small victories seemed less than trivial. The troopers weren't ready for action. And so he was deeply concerned when he received the official communiqué from Nouméa telling him to alert his command for embarkation. He knew now that it was all true and that the push was to be staged in Cape Gloucester. It would be a tough campaign. And he did not expect, for one minute, that his men would be there to assist.

They had not been very well treated either by himself or by the general, the major reasoned. Burgermeister discriminated against them, as was manifest in the bulletin denying them permission to see their favorite actress when she came to entertain the troops of the island. One of Barrow's first acts as their new commanding officer had been to declare an all-out war against them in an effort to destroy their spirit—to remold them into the type of Marines he had envisaged after studying his cold, impersonal Book. No one gave the paratroopers a break, and even the way they were advised of their up-coming participation in the invasion was delivered in such a way as to antagonize and hurt them.

And their unique outlook on anything military served to strengthen Barrow's misgivings. They were not heroes —at least to themselves. They wanted to go about their business, drink their Stump Juice cocktails, flirt with the girls, and turn a buck. They must have changed greatly during the time between Guadalcanal and their new invasion orders. They did not impress Barrow as crack combat troops. They did not even impress Barrow as dependable troops—and he blamed himself.

"If I had been more understanding," he thought, punishing himself, "they would be ready for this battle —at least psychologically."

And so, each morning after the news had been delivered to the men, Major Barrow timorously entered the company streets, expecting to see them deserted, the men gone and hiding in the hills of New Caledonia. He was almost sure, after hearing the latest additions to the "Marine's Hymn," that they would go over the hill in a body.

Worried and depressed, he walked through his beloved area for the final time. He noticed that even on the eve of an embarkation—or desertion—the men kept their tents and streets immaculate. As usual their pyramidals were orderly and their bunks tautly made. But in the last tents on the street, he again could see that the beds were unmade, the shapely legs of Marie Belanger busily working around them as she tucked in the sheets and blankets.

Here was the one friend who had remained constantly loyal to him and the troopers, Barrow realized. Her good sense had gotten him and the troopers out of one serious crisis after another. It was this lovely girl who had offered herself as hostage so that Kathy Kennedy could be returned to Nouméa in time to keep the paratroopers from suffering the terrible retribution of the infuriated general. In fact, it was Marie who had hit upon the scheme to "rescue" the actress. And she had even conspired with the paratroopers against her own father so that the wrath of the French general would not be visited upon them.

Major Barrow entered the tent where Marie Belanger was working, and sat on the edge of an unmade bed. Marie paused in her work to listen to his good-bye.

"I'm leaving tomorrow, Marie," the major stated.

"I know."

"I want to thank you for everything you did for us."

"You're welcome."

Without wishing to do so, Barrow again remembered the occasion when he had led the girl through the streets of the battalion while her father searched for her.

"I'm sorry about that time . . ." he began.

"Don't be sorry for anything," the girl interrupted, sitting down beside him. "I've never been so happy as I have been with you and the men. I've had a grand time and I loved every minute of it."

"We think you're wonderful," Barrow said sincerely.

"I love every one of you," Marie replied.

"Marie . . ." Barrow went on hesitantly.

"Yes?"

"On the day that I left you in the Kanaka village as hostage for Miss Kennedy, I started to tell you something. It's important that I convey to you . . ."

"Please," she interrupted, "don't be so pompous."

"I'm not being pompous."

"I think you were about to tell me that you loved me that day in the native village."

"I did. How did you know?"

"It doesn't make any difference. Would you like to tell me now?"

"Yes," he said awkwardly. "And maybe after the invasion . . ."

"I'll be waiting here for you."

"Hey, look at that," the loud voice of Corporal Crocker intruded as Barrow tried to be tender with the girl he loved. "Major Barrow is kissing Marie on an enlisted man's bed."

"He ought to kiss her on a commissioned bed," Pfc. Howes said as he joined the rapidly gathering group of Marines.

"He shouldn't be carrying on like that in broad daylight." First Sergeant Maxwellington was critical.

"Excuse me, Major." Corporal Martin advanced. "Would you like me to roll down the sides of the tent? You're embarrassing the enlisted men."

"Proceed, Corporal."

Early the next morning Barrow bravely formed the words he would deliver to the general who would wait in vain for the paratroopers to take their place aboard the troop transport. He would explain that General Burgermeister shared his blame for the desertion of the men. And then Barrow would volunteer for service with another combat force.

And so he was not prepared for the roll call that was held that morning before the men filed aboard the U.S.S. *Heywood*, their transport. That was the day he got a whole new philosophy of life.

"I've had the quartermaster lay out six extra heavy marching orders," First Sergeant Maxwellington reported.

"Six extra?"

"Yes, sir." Maxwellington paused. "And you know, I think this new Marine Corps has the old one put to shame."

"But why the six extra issues of gear?" Barrow prodded.

Maxwellington handed Barrow the results of the roll call, and the major hurried to inspect his men and confirm the roll.

It was true.

Corporal Masterson had abandoned his berth as commanding officer of the Tontouta strip and taken his place in the ranks alongside Private Williams, late first sergeant of the Casual and Replacement Battalion. Burgermeister had compromised and awarded Pfc. Checkoway the Silver Star so that he could be released from the brig to go along on the hit. He stood beside Private Hession, who had left his desirable position as a member of the consular detachment in New Zealand, where he served with his father-in-law, the Minister of Defense. Sergeant Schmidt turned up in civilian clothes. He had just flown in from Brisbane, Australia. Four men reported in from Wellington and Auckland. Private Cannizero had hopped ships all the way down from Guadalcanal, where he had been on the firing line with the Army replacements. Two nuts had sent wires that they could be picked up on Tulagi, and one trooper had showed up in a sailor suit. He had conned his way aboard the *Big Mo* and had set up an ice-cream stand. Admiral Dorsey raised hell and wanted him back. Three chutists had broken out of the First Guard Company's brig and joined the ranks with the Pfc. who had married a native girl and set up house-keeping in the mountains. The best one of all, though, was Corporal Sampson, who came all the way back from San Francisco, where he had established a thriving taxi business.

"It was a perfect roll call," Maxwellington said, breathless himself. "Two hundred and nine men present, six more than we have on the books."

The proudest major in the United States Marine Corps led his men in review before General Burgermeister as they approached the troopship.

"How that man has changed," Colonel Ward said to the general, pointing out the tall and straight major. "Those troopers didn't tear him apart after all."

"No," Burgermeister agreed. "They got together and tore me apart."

"Magnificent men," General Belanger said admiringly of the paratroopers. "Wonderful leadership. The discerning major will become a colonel if this war lasts long enough."

"He'll become a general," Marie amended. "You wouldn't want to outrank your son-in-law."

Belanger shot a startled but happy look at his lovely daughter, and then, with his eyes, followed the dashing Marine officer who had expressed such admiration for the beloved General De Gaulle. "Marie," he cried, "you are going to marry Major Barrow?"

She nodded proudly.

Belanger put his arm across the shoulder of his daughter. "I'm glad. You have made me the happiest man in New Caledonia."

Marie blushed slightly as she recalled the wonderful details of her hour with Major Barrow in the pyramidal tent after the corporal had rolled down the sides. "The *second* happiest man in New Caledonia," she quietly corrected her father.

ROBERT G. FULLER was born in Newburyport, Massachusetts, in 1921. He is now right back where he started—but in the intervening years he and his family have journeyed through forty-six states, and all over Canada and Cuba. Six months were spent in Guadalajara, Mexico, and three times in the past three years Mr. Fuller has lived and worked in California.

He joined the Marine Corps in 1939 as a private, and was discharged five years later as a private. While in the Corps he was awarded a Navy Cross (America's second highest decoration for heroism), the Purple Heart and other medals. Like the characters in DAN-GER! MARINES AT WORK! he served as a para-marine in the First Parachute Battalion, First Marine Division. He saw action on Guadalcanal and other islands in the Solomons during the first offensives of World War II.

After his discharge, Mr. Fuller worked as a long-shoreman, but left the waterfront to attend Boston University, where he received his bachelor of science in Journalism. Armed with his precious degree, he worked in a shoebox factory, on a construction labor gang, as an engineering aide, as a minimum-wage investigator and as an assistant sales promotion manager.

Mr. Fuller's short stories have appeared in magazines over the past ten years. DANGER! MARINES AT WORK! is his first book. It will soon be followed by another.

Mr. Fuller is married and has two children, a son and a daughter.